Pretty Freekin Scary™

You Smell
~Dead~

P9-DGH-578

Special thanks to Nancy Holder
for bringing this book to life.

GROSSET & DUNLAP
Published by the Penguin Group
Penguin Group (USA) Inc., 375 Hudson Street, New York, New York 10014, USA
Penguin Group (Canada), 90 Eglinton Avenue East, Suite 700, Toronto,
Ontario M4P 2Y3, Canada
(a division of Pearson Penguin Canada Inc.)
Penguin Books Ltd., 80 Strand, London WC2R 0RL, England
Penguin Group Ireland, 25 St. Stephen's Green, Dublin 2, Ireland
(a division of Penguin Books Ltd.)
Penguin Group (Australia), 250 Camberwell Road, Camberwell, Victoria 3124, Australia
(a division of Pearson Australia Group Pty. Ltd.)
Penguin Books India Pvt. Ltd., 11 Community Centre, Panchsheel Park,
New Delhi—110 017, India
Penguin Group (NZ), 67 Apollo Drive, Rosedale, North Shore 0745, Auckland, New Zealand
(a division of Pearson New Zealand Ltd.)
Penguin Books (South Africa) (Pty.) Ltd., 24 Sturdee Avenue,
Rosebank, Johannesburg 2196, South Africa

Penguin Books Ltd., Registered Offices: 80 Strand, London WC2R 0RL, England

Pretty Freekin Scary™ and related trademarks © 2007 AGC, Inc. Used under license by
Penguin Young Readers Group. All rights reserved. Published by Grosset & Dunlap, a division
of Penguin Young Readers Group, 345 Hudson Street, New York, New York 10014.
GROSSET & DUNLAP is a trademark of Penguin Group (USA) Inc. Printed in the U.S.A.

Library of Congress Control Number: 2007010827

ISBN 978-0-448-44682-0   10 9 8 7 6 5 4 3 2 1

Pretty Freekin Scary™

You Smell Dead

a novel by
Chris P. Flesh

Grosset & Dunlap

Chapter One:

In Which We Meet Our Hero, Freekin

Welcome, Gentle Reader, to this book. I am Your Humble Yet Rather Desperate Narrator. You see, until recently I was narrating the chronicles of some truly amazing individuals. People I admired and respected. Humanitarians, artists, and captains of industry.

It was an honor to have the opportunity to work with such luminaries, but it was felt by some that I had

"gotten underfoot." That I had interfered in their lives! That I had invaded their privacy! *That I had asked too many questions.*

And so, I was unjustly booted out of the International Order of Narrators and told never to narrate again. Is it even possible to imagine the depth of my complete and utter shock? My horror? My dismay?

I was on the verge of a nervous collapse. I didn't know what to do with myself. All this talent, all this natural curiosity, wasting away. And then . . . I came upon the heartwarming yet gut-wrenching tale of a boy named Franklin Ripp. Gentle Reader, what I learned was shocking. Riveting. Mesmerizing. I connected to his story right away. Perhaps because I saw a bit of myself in young Franklin. After all, he's so very much like me—talented, curious, and wasting away! And I knew that I could tell his story without getting underfoot, invading his privacy, or asking too many questions. (I really could.)

So, here it is, my macabre masterpiece. I am certain that once the International Order of Narrators has read this tale of excitement and despair, hope and then more despair, they will welcome me back with open arms, apologies, and, hopefully, a nice plaque or a shiny medal.

There is just one small problem, Gentle Reader, and

here it is: I have been unable to persuade the International Order of Narrators to actually read my terrifying tome. Last month, I sent them a copy of this story, and I received it back unopened. The words DELIVERY REFUSED were written across the front of the package. It shouldn't surprise you to learn that I was once again nearly overwhelmed with dismay and, yes, yet more despair.

And so I make this appeal to you, My Very Dear Reader: If, after you finish this Humble Book, you are as astonished and entertained as I sincerely hope you will be, I beg you to contact the International Order of Narrators and tell them so. Perhaps if they receive enough letters praising this effort, they will finally read it, and my dreams of a second chance will come true.

Once I am reinstated, I can promise you additional exciting, hopeful, despairing stories about Franklin and his own attempts to have a second chance. But until such time, I may be forced to earn my living through more traditional channels than narrating. By flipping burgers at the local McDonald's restaurant or bagging groceries at the Piggly Wiggly. But let us not, as you young people say, *go there*, shall we?

Come with me now to the town of Snickering Willows—the birthplace of young Franklin, who will in time assume the name of Freekin.

Snickering Willows was founded in 1889 by Horatio Snickering III. You may know Mr. Snickering as the inventor of Mystery Meat, that strange gray mass found bubbling and boiling in the cooking vats of school cafeterias, where it is then smothered inside taco shells or drowned in marinara sauce and sold as food.

Back in 1889, nearly everyone in the tiny village of Snickering Willows worked at the Mystery Meat kitchen, a simple wooden building on the edge of town. Mr. Snickering himself stirred the vat of Top Secret Ingredients . . . in the dead of night, when no one else was there.

Whatever the Top Secret Ingredients were, they proved irresistible to diners everywhere. Mystery Meat was an overnight sensation. It was so popular that in less than a year, Mr. Snickering became rich. He expanded the modest wooden kitchen into an enormous factory, which loomed like a hulking gargoyle behind twisted metal gates bearing his name. Day and night, smoke and steam belched from its copper pipes and tilted towers, while enormous crates of Mystery Meat bobbled along creaking conveyer belts into wagons, train cars, and barges, destined for the cafeterias of schools all over the world—including the one you currently attend, I would imagine.

4

The little village transformed into a town, which Mr. Snickering owned lock, stock, and barrel: His name was on the deeds of all the buildings rented out to businesses, the railroad station, the utility company, and the land on which all the houses were built. It came as no surprise that he was elected the town's first mayor. Some called him a king.

Others, a dictator.

Under his watchful eye, the citizens of Snickering Willows enjoyed remarkable prosperity. Everyone had a job, a place to live, and money to buy every newfangled invention that came along—motorcars, telephones, and leisure time. Their children were pudgy and well fed. Their senior citizens lived to a ripe old age.

But there was a problem: People love a good mystery, and to solve them even more. Everyone in Snickering Willows wanted to know what was *in* the Mystery Meat. Rumors abounded regarding the Top Secret Ingredients. Local chefs attempted to recreate Mystery Meat in their private kitchens. Rival businessmen tried to steal the secret recipe so they could sell competing brands for less.

In 1890, Elias Snorting started selling Betcha Can't Guess Beef. In 1891, Wilhelmina Trotter created Furtive Furters. But none of the imitations tasted as good as Mystery Meat.

The questions persisted: "What's in it? Why does it taste so good?" Horatio Snickering III knew that these were dangerous questions. If they were answered, the entire economy of Snickering Willows would collapse. He became obsessed by the idea that no one dare so much as ask, for perhaps someone would be tricked into answering. No matter that he, and he alone, knew the secret recipe. Someday he would die, and so someone else would have to know; and perhaps the next keeper of the secret would not be as vigilant as he.

He lay awake nights thinking of the many ways such questions could be phrased:

1. As I am allergic to: peanuts, soy, lactose, shellfish, strawberries, cheddar cheese, and 2,612 other foods, listed in alphabetical order in the small document I am now handing to you, do you suppose I will break out in hives if I dine on Mystery Meat?

2. Do you know that I am the prince of a far-off land, and I will make you a baron if you will divulge the Top Secret Ingredients?

3. If you want to see your child again in this lifetime, would you please be so kind as to write down the recipe, and leave it by the statue of Horatio Snickering III in the center of Snickering Willows Municipal Park at eleven o'clock tonight?

It was obvious to him that by answering any number

of seemingly innocent questions, someone could actually reveal the Top Secret Ingredients. Worrying about it drove him nearly insane—some say he *did* go insane. Whatever the case, on New Year's Day, January 1, 1891, Mayor Horatio Snickering III issued a decree:

Whosoever shall reside in or visit the town of Snickering Willows shall not ask questions on any subject, at any time, for any reason. Anyone found asking a question shall be found guilty of Curiosity, and shall be escorted to the town border, and not be permitted to cross back over it. Any member of the community found to be in contact with a convicted Questioner shall likewise be exiled from Snickering Willows forever.

Yes, Gentle Reader, Horatio Snickering III actually declared it a crime to ask a question. In the next week, 337 people were arrested for Curiosity, and 312 of them departed Snickering Willows forever.

Of course, large numbers of indignant citizens chose to leave Snickering Willows voluntarily, rather than submit to such a ridiculous law. But many more deemed it a small price to pay for a comfortable lifestyle, and left their Curiosity behind forever. What was at first a new law soon became a habit. Eventually it was as if the descendants of the original Snickering Willowites were born without the ability to ask questions. It may seem difficult to believe, but by the time Franklin Ripp died, he had never asked a question in his entire life.

So there it is.

Now we begin our story, with Franklin Ripp but three seconds away from death—

—*one Mississippi*—

—which he could have avoided, if only he had asked a few simple questions, such as these. (And these are only *examples* of what the questions could have been—not the actual questions themselves. I must tell you that I promised him I wouldn't reveal the cause of his death. It is *his* secret, and I must say that if I had died the same way, I wouldn't want anyone to know, either. It was a humiliating, ridiculous, completely unnecessary way to go, and if I were at liberty to tell you about it, it's quite likely you would burst out laughing until you cried. As such, no one among the living but his parents knows the cause, and I have made a solemn vow to Franklin that I would carry that secret to my own grave, and as I am a Narrator who can be trusted utterly by the main characters of my stories, I shall do just that.)

(Though not anytime soon, I hope.)

1. Is this safe?

2. Has anyone ever tried this before?

3. Is it the second rail or the third?

—*two Mississippi*—

But because he lived in Snickering Willows, Franklin didn't ask any questions at all.

—*three Mississippi!*

And so he died.

Chapter Two:
In Which Our Hero Unleashes His Curiosity

"Why?" Franklin demanded. He stomped back and forth in front of the towering ebony desks of the three members of the Afterlife Commission. Although he'd only been dead for one brief summer, he felt as if he had been dead for years.

"Why did you take me so early?"

It was a question he had asked the Commission at

least 123 times. Having lived a life of never asking any questions at all, ever, he was nearly overcome by the pent-up energy of his curiosity. He bombarded the Commissioners with hundreds of questions a day, but "Why did you take me so early?" was his favorite, and the one he asked most often.

"Why, why, *why?*" he demanded, staring up at the Commissioners with his green eyes. Ms. Totenbone, Monsieur DeMise, and Lord Grym-Reaper peered down at him as he pounded his fist against a desk, his black hair flopping to and fro. The sound of whispers and giggles came from the other side of the door. It was Pretty and Scary, Franklin's two friends from the Underworld. Pretty was a million-year-old monster, and Scary was her timid little buddy—a shape-shifting phantom. Franklin had met them after his very first meeting with the Commission. He'd just sort of woken up, and the Commissioners had explained to him that he was dead and ought to find a job and a place to dwell as soon as possible. He'd been so upset, he had slammed out of the hearing room and stalked down a mist-filled corridor. Then another. And another.

Lost, he went down a flight of stairs—and a few more, and more—not realizing until it was too late that he had actually traveled nearly thirteen miles below the surface of the Afterlife, to the dark, dreary, and even weirder Underworld. Monsters of all varieties lived there, including one made out of purple goo, and another that was nothing but scraggly white hair. Most of them had big teeth and claws, and they chased him through the cold black landscape, growling and roaring.

And while he was running *away* from them, he ran *into* Pretty and Scary. Pretty had never seen a human boy before, and she squeezed him nearly in two and shouted, "You so pretty!"

Then she growled at the monsters bearing down on Franklin. Her ponytail ears went rigid. Fire erupted from her half-circle mouth, which glistened with dozens of tiny teeth. And her eyes spun. All seven of them.

"GALAGABALOO!" Pretty screamed, and the other monsters panicked and scattered.

Scary turned himself into a bolt of lightning and hurled himself at the retreating Underworlders as they fled into the darkness, never to return.

"Thanks, um . . ." Franklin said.

"Pretty. Me so Pretty," she replied. She pointed to the small creature floating beside her in the air. "He so Scary."

"Nice to meet you. I'm Franklin," he said.

Cooing, Pretty grabbed Franklin again and kissed him

at least two hundred times on his cheek. Scary fluttered against his other cheek. Then, as Pretty sang to herself, Franklin found the stairs back up to the Afterlife.

He thanked them again and got ready to say good-bye, but Pretty decided she couldn't bear to part from him. They'd stayed with him ever since, sticking so close that he felt almost as if he had found a replacement for Sophie, his beloved dog.

Actually, that was kind of how the Afterlifers viewed the two Underworlders—like Franklin's pets, who weren't allowed into places like Afterlife Commission hearings.

"I was just about to have my best year ever. I had it *all*," Franklin reminded the Commissioners. He could hear Pretty giggling and whispering behind the door, and Scary gibbering back at her in Phantomese, his native language.

He ran his fingers through his hair and dropped his arms to his sides.

"Well, I *almost* had it all," he amended. "I was going to try out for the football team; and Steve Johnson and I had just started our band, and Lilly Weezbrock—"

Ms. Totenbone, who sat in the middle, groaned and lowered her forehead to her desk with a clack. She was a skeleton with red hair wound high on top of her skull and makeup slathered all over her cheekbones and eye

sockets. "Here we go again," she said. Her teeth chattered when she talked. "Lilly, Lilly, Lilly. Franklin, how many times have we told you to just move on? You died. Let your old life go."

"That's just it. Why don't *you* get it? I didn't have a chance to live my life." He stopped pacing and flung out his arms. "You took me too soon. I died before I was supposed to. Why can't you just admit you made a mistake?"

"Oh, Franklin, you ask so many questions. Over and over and over again," Ms. Totenbone said.

Lord Grym-Reaper silently bowed his hooded head, as if to agree. But Monsieur DeMise was listening carefully to every word Franklin said. Which is quite an accomplishment for someone whose mass consists mostly of lesions and sores.

"Do you know that I'm from Snickering Willows?" Franklin asked them. "Do you even know what it's like there? People *never* ask questions, ever. I had a question on the tip of my tongue just before I died, and I didn't ask it. And I probably *wouldn't* have died if I *had* asked it. So I've learned my lesson. If I have a question, I'm asking it."

"Not in this hearing room," Ms. Totenbone insisted. "Case dismissed *again*."

"*Non, non*, wait," Monsieur DeMise said, raising his gooey hands for attention—or perhaps something to wipe them on. "I am having ze second thoughts. Zis great life Franklin speaks of. It comes down to one thing: ze true love." He cocked his head as he looked down at Franklin. "You really want to reunite with Mademoiselle Weezbrock. Am I correct?"

Franklin nodded, trying not to blush (before remembering that he couldn't).

"Ah, you see?" Monsieur DeMise slammed his hands on his desk. When he lifted them up, pieces of flesh stuck to the wood. "He was about to claim her with ze kiss of ze love, just like in ze fairy tales and old movies. And then, poof! He is dead, and it is too late."

"That's too bad," Ms. Totenbone said firmly.

"Ah, *mes amis*, it is a tragedy!" Monsieur DeMise cried. "Surely we can send him back to claim zat kiss. He has ze unfinished business."

"Right!" Franklin cried.

"He had his chance," Ms. Totenbone insisted.

"But how can we stand in ze way of ze love?" Monsieur DeMise protested. "For ze sake of lovers everywhere, I insist zat we bend ze rule, just for zis once."

"Just this once," Franklin pleaded.

Ms. Totenbone lowered her head to her desk again.

Then she raised it, tilted it back, and let out a low, slow breath like a leaky balloon. She looked to her left at Lord Grym-Reaper, who shrugged. She looked at Monsieur DeMise, who nodded eagerly.

"All right, already," Ms. Totenbone said. "You win."

Franklin blinked at her. He stared at the three of them, each in turn. It was so unexpected, and so much what he wanted to hear, that he couldn't quite believe it.

"I win?" he repeated.

"Yes," she replied. She sounded less than pleased.

"You'll send me back?"

"Yes. We'll send you back."

"Sweet!" Franklin cried.

From behind the door, Pretty wailed, "No, no, no! Pretty does not want!"

"*Gagaliebu,*" Scary whimpered.

"On one condition. You'll have the school year to achieve this great life you insist we snatched you away from," Ms. Totenbone continued, ignoring Pretty and Scary, as many often did.

"To kiss ze beautiful Lilly Weezbrock," Monsieur DeMise clarified.

"Yes. To kiss Lilly." Ms. Totenbone flipped the pages of a large appointment book on her desk. "Let's see.

The last day of the current school year is Friday, June thirteenth. Interesting. It is also the anniversary of your death."

"An auspicious date," Monsieur DeMise said.

"If, by that date," Ms. Totenbone continued, "you have nothing to show for your second chance—no kiss— you'll die again."

"And we may even send you to a worse place than this," Lord Grym-Reaper added sternly. His gravelly, echoing voice made Franklin's skin crawl. "I want to go on record as protesting this decision. We've never done it before, and I think it sets a bad example to other dead young people."

"Duly noted, and agreed," Ms. Totenbone said.

She leaned forward on her elbows and stared down at Franklin. "So, Franklin. Do we have a deal?"

"Yes," Franklin said. "I'll prove to you that I was supposed to stay alive." *For Lilly.*

"We'll look for that proof," Ms. Totenbone said. "June thirteenth. Be ready." A gavel appeared in her right hand. "By the power vested in me, I send you back to the Land of the Living." She raised the gavel.

Franklin took a deep breath and braced himself. He had no idea what it was going to feel like.

At the same instant, Pretty flung the door open so

hard that it ripped right off the hinges and crashed to the floor. Her tentacles flailed as she shot across the room. Her seven eyes bulged with horror. Her rows of little teeth flashed as she let out a wail of full-bore anguish.

"No!" she begged, waving her arms. Her ponytail ears bobbed wildly. "Pretty need Franklin!"

Behind her, Scary shape-shifted into a trembling lower lip.

"Wawa," Scary bawled.

"What a scene," Lord Grym-Reaper sniffed.

"Your year starts now," Ms. Totenbone announced as she slammed the gavel down sharply on her desk.

"No!" Pretty shrieked.

In an instant, everything went black as death, and silent as the grave.

And Franklin woke up, as if from a nasty dream . . .

. . . buried six feet under, inside his moldy coffin.

Chapter Three:
In Which Our Hero Rises from the Grave

"Hey, wait a minute! This isn't fair!" Franklin shouted. Lying flat on his back, he balled his fists and pounded on the inside of the lid, which was covered with slime green satin. The rotten wood easily gave way, and clouds of dirt smacked his cheeks and forehead.

Sputtering, he wiped them away, and that was when he saw that he had not only been sent back into his moldy

coffin, but into his moldy corpse as well. He had been dead for almost three months, and his earthly body had been busily rotting away all that time. Formaldehyde can only accomplish so much. His left thumb was covered with fungus, and black goo was oozing from the knuckle of his right thumb.

"Gah! I'm a monster!" Franklin screamed.

"Gagzeebili!" Scary whispered happily as he passed through the bottom of the coffin and fluttered nose to nose with Franklin. The little phantom cooed.

Then the entire left side of the coffin burst apart as Pretty shot up from the earth below. "Franklin is not monster!" she shrieked maniacally into his ear, throwing her arms around Franklin's neck. Bones cracked. But there was no pain. "Franklin is Pretty's favorite boy *ever*! Cutie-pie!" She kissed his cheek about two hundred times and squeezed him harder.

More bones cracked. It still didn't hurt.

"Oh, no, you can't be here," Franklin grunted, trying to pry her hands from around his throat and dodge her slobbery kisses.

"Pretty needs Franklin!" she insisted. "Scary, too!"

"Gazizii!" Scary twirled in a circle, no small feat in the narrow space.

Before Franklin could reply, Pretty looked around at

the ruined coffin, then ticked her gaze back to Franklin and shook her head.

"Pretty does not like Land of the Living. Too small. Franklin said there's a mall. Franklin said there are churros."

Franklin had spent a lot of time reminiscing about Snickering Willows. Clearly, Pretty had hung on every word.

"This isn't the Land of the Living," he said.

He grabbed at a loose piece of the coffin lid and broke it off. Shreds of slime green satin floated down like soggy radioactive snowflakes. "It's up there."

"Ooh!" Pretty clapped her hands. "Take Pretty there, Franklin!"

She threw back her head and began gnawing on the underside of the lid. Scary morphed into a glowing red exit sign, and then a blinking yellow arrow.

I can't go back like this, Franklin thought. *I'm dead. Well, not exactly. Maybe . . . undead?*

Pretty kept gnawing. Scary pulsed and glowed. All Franklin could do was imagine Lilly's look of horror when she saw him again.

The government will take me away to study me. Or I'll get put in quarantine, or an insane asylum. Maybe they'll try to dissect me.

Or maybe once I reach the surface, I'll go back to normal. No matter what, I can't take these two with me.

He tapped Pretty on the shoulder. "Is there a way back to the Afterlife?" He turned over on his side and tried to peer into the hole she'd made in the coffin floor. All he saw was darkness.

"You want *back?*" she asked, disbelieving. "Franklin begged and begged *please-please-please let me go.*"

"I meant a way for *you,*" he explained. "So *you* could go back."

"*Pretty?*" Her two largest eyes grew huge. The five smaller ones blinked. "Pretty go back?"

"Yeah, because you're a monster from the Underworld, and—"

"Pretty can*not* leave Franklin." She shook her head. Her ponytail ears bounced and bobbled.

"*Gazilulu,*" Scary added. He fluttered his wings close to Franklin's cheek.

"Look, I like you guys, too," Franklin said, "but I'm sure the Commissioners didn't want you to leave with me." At least, he hoped not.

"Pretty is here," she insisted. "Scary is here."

"*Baleei,*" Scary murmured, bobbing up and down.

Franklin tried again. "I'm going to have enough trouble fitting in without you guys."

Pretty's smile faded. "Trouble?"

"Yeah, because we don't have undead kids in Snickering Willows. Or . . . monsters. Seriously, I had it going on when I was . . . completely alive. My best friend and I had just started our band, and I was a highly respected skateboarder. Plus, I had Lilly. Almost. But now I'm undead, and it's going to be weird for me, and you'll just make it weirder."

"*Weirder?!*" Pretty's voice was strangled. Her little shoulders hunched, her head drooped, and she made a high squealing sound like a rusty gate.

She was crying.

"*Wawa*, Pretty." Scary turned into a handkerchief and flew beneath her lowered face, wiping her many eyes.

"I didn't mean you were weird," Franklin lied. "It's just . . ." He didn't even know where to start. "Just that you . . ." He sighed. He couldn't bear to hurt her. "Okay. You can stay."

Pretty squealed and clapped her hands. "Me so happy now!"

Now he'd done it. He still clung to the hope that they wouldn't be able to leave his grave, since they were Underworlders. "As long as you stay out of sight. And behave."

"Okie-dokie! Heave ho, Franklin!"

Humming to herself, Pretty finished chewing through the top of Franklin's coffin and began tunneling her way through the dirt. Scary morphed into a set of blades and whirled in a circle, widening the passageway for Franklin. Soon the clumps of dirt gave way to a layer of mud wriggling with earthworms and gleaming with the occasional human skull.

Oh my God, Franklin thought, *this cannot be happening. It is just too gross. But worth it if it leads to a reunion with my Lilly.*

Pretty broke through the surface first. She scrabbled out and planted herself on the gentle rise of Franklin's grave, bending at the waist and stretching out her hands to him.

"Come, Franklin!" she sang. "Pretty can help!"

He put his hands in Pretty's and worked his way out of the hole. It wasn't long before he was standing on top of his own grave, staring at his own square marble headstone.

FRANKLIN RIPP, BELOVED SON

"You got that right," he murmured.

Franklin stared past his headstone to the swaying limbs of a weeping willow tree. Stars twinkled and shone,

and a crescent moon hung low in the velvety sky. The whisper of polluted air from the belching chimneys of the Snickering Willows Mystery Meat factory riffled the tatters of his burial pajamas.

I'm really back! I just rose from my own grave!

"We're going to leave," he told them. "We're going to my house. We'll stick to the shadows."

"Franklin so sticky!" Pretty cried as she pushed her fingertips against a lesion on his face. Sure enough, they stuck. He *was* sticky. If he tried to kiss Lilly . . . He grimaced at the image of their two faces plastered together.

Then he thought back to the last day of school—the day before he had died. He'd worked up his courage for weeks, swearing to himself that he would kiss her on the last day of school. He hadn't slept at all the night before. He had tossed and turned, wondering what it would be like to touch the lips of Lilly Weezbrock with his own.

The last bell of the entire school year rang. Everyone burst out the school doors, including Franklin and Lilly.

"Finally!" she cried. "It's over!"

Finally, he thought. *I'm going to kiss you.*

He could still see her dark blue eyes and her encouraging smile, smell her vanilla perfume as he moved closer, closer . . .

Lilly closed her eyes and parted her lips.

He was just a hair's breadth away . . .

Lilly lifted her chin.

I'm going to kiss her. I am actually going to press my lips against her lips and . . . what if I have bad breath? Or BO? What if I burp or . . . worse?

I want to kiss her. I should kiss her. I will kiss her!

Later. Another time.

He pulled away and she opened her eyes, surprised and disappointed.

Do it. Just do it, he ordered himself. *Look at her. She wants you to. Look at her . . .*

She's so beautiful. I must be crazy, thinking she wants me to kiss her. She's not disappointed. I'm making that all up. She's just standing there, like a normal, pretty girl.

If I try, she'll just laugh. Or she'll hate me forever. I'd die if Lilly hated me. I'd rather get run over by a truck. Or eat poison, or . . .

She's still here, dude. She wants *you to!*

Summoning every ounce of courage he had, he leaned toward her again. She smiled, closed her eyes once more, and leaned in toward him . . .

"Yo, Weezy!" Deirdre, Lilly's best friend, waved to her from across the street.

Lilly opened her eyes.

No! Franklin thought. *Ignore her!*

Deidre waved at Lilly. "C'mon! Let's go!"

No! No, no, no!

"Gotta go," Lilly said to him, in a breathy, warm whisper. "We're going to a cheerleading party." She smiled shyly. "Catch you later!"

Kiss you later, he had thought as he watched her jog across the street. He'd totally blown it! *I will make up for it. I will, I will. I will kiss you, Lilly, if that's the last thing I ever do.*

But he had died instead.

Yes, Gentle Reader, died in that humiliating, heinous, hideous, horrendous manner I have sworn not to reveal, as it is so mortifying, and morbidly amusing, and shame-inducing, that I would not wish it on my greatest enemy . . . or the person who refused the delivery of this manuscript.

But now I have another chance, Franklin thought. *I'll kiss Lilly Weezbrock, or die trying.*

Franklin kept to the shadows, and about half an hour after he had crawled out of his grave, he was home. It was almost too good for Franklin to believe.

Should I go look for Lilly first? No, my parents would kill me if I didn't check in first. So to speak.

"Hi, honey, we're home!" Pretty yodeled.

"Shh," he told her. "I don't want to wake them up. See that old willow tree? We're going to climb it to get to that window." He pointed to his bedroom window.

"Okie-dokie!" Pretty said.

Scary just flew around Franklin's head like a goldfish in a bowl as Franklin climbed and Pretty sort of slithered.

Once they were inside, the moonlight poured through the window, and Franklin decided not to turn on the light. He could see that his room was exactly as he had left it. His bed was even made up with sheets and a light summer blanket. His guitar still lay on his study desk, beside his arrangement for a new ballad about Lilly that he'd been working on: "Cheerleading Queen." A note from Steve was still tacked to his computer monitor. It was dated June twelfth, and said, "Practice tomorrow, my house, ten AM!" *Creepy.*

Franklin moved to the ten large photos of Lilly, which made up the bulk of the Wall of Lilly. It also included a few pieces of crepe paper from one of her cheerleading pompoms and a bubble gum wrapper she'd touched.

"Lilly?" Pretty demanded, pressing her eyes against Franklin's favorite picture of Lilly. Dressed in her cheerleader outfit, she was standing on her tiptoes beside the team mascot, pretending to take a bite out of him. The Snickering Willows sports teams were the

Carnivores, and their mascot was Meaty Mouse.

"Shh," Franklin cautioned her, nodding. His ear was cocked for Sophie's barking. "Yes. That's Lilly."

"Not Pretty," she informed him. She snaked her fingers underneath the picture. "Me throw out!"

"No!" he whispered loudly. "Don't touch anything. This is my stuff. My room. You're just a guest."

"Humph." Pretty snaked her hand back down and flounced over to his guitar. "This is churros?" She grabbed the guitar by the neck and prepared to chomp down on it.

"No!" He eased it away from her. "It's not churros. I have no churros. This is a guitar. I'm in a band. We call ourselves the 50-50s." He gestured to a photo tacked just above his computer monitor. There were five guys in the picture, all holding skateboards—Otter, Hal, Jamie, Franklin, and Steve.

Chubby, red-haired Steve towered over the other guys, and he outweighed everyone else by at least fifty pounds. Steve wasn't all that great a boarder, but he practiced hard and had a lot of heart. Kind of like Franklin and his guitar. Steve was a much better player than he was. They'd gotten together last year to play at the talent show, and that was when they'd decided to form the 50-50s. The band was named for the skateboarding term for hopping onto and off of things, like the railing of Daredevil

Bridge, which spanned Dead Man's Creek.

"See that big guy? That's Steve, my best friend."

Pretty fluttered her lashes at him. "Pretty and Scary Franklin's best friends."

"Right. From the Afterlife," he said with a faint smile as he reached out and playfully tugged one of her ears. She giggled and clacked her teeth. Even though she was ancient, she was like a little kid.

"Gazu," Scary gibbered sweetly.

Franklin went to his closet and felt around on the floor. Sure enough, his trusty skateboard was still there.

Scary swooped over to Franklin's bed. *"Gazika?"*

"I don't speak Phantomese," Franklin reminded him, holding the board and spinning a wheel.

"Scary says, beddy-bye?" Pretty explained. "Franklin's sleepy?"

He wasn't. He was anything but. And he wanted to go into the bathroom to see exactly what he looked like.

But he didn't want to wake up his parents. He thought it would be less . . . terrifying . . . if they saw him in daylight. And the truth was, he was afraid to see what his face looked like.

What if my parents run screaming from the house when they see me? Maybe they'll *be the ones to hand me over to the government to dissect.*

But I have to let them know I'm back. Daylight will be better. Hey, maybe I'll go back to normal tonight!

Nervous and anxious, he put his skateboard back in the closet, then lay down on his mattress. Pretty made a nest of towels at the foot of his bed. Scary turned himself into a little stuffed doll and Pretty clutched him under her arm, curled up, and started snoring. Scary fell asleep, too, with a soft little smile on his face.

Franklin lay for most of the night with his hands across his chest, staring at the ceiling. *I probably look like a corpse,* he thought finally, unfolding his hands and laying them at his sides. *What will Lilly say when she sees me?*

He smiled just thinking about her. And his ears began to tingle.

Chapter Four:
In Which Our Hero Stifles His Curiosity

As the sun lightened his bedroom, Franklin gradually became aware of the smell of bacon, which was much better than the way *he* smelled.

I reek! And my room stinks like something died in it!

"*Galoo?*" Scary asked, yawning and slipping from beneath Pretty's arm.

"I have to go talk to my parents," Franklin told him,

sitting up. *It's now or . . . maybe I could wait another day. Or two. Or never let anyone know.*

No. If I have any hope of proving my life is worth living, people need to know I'm here, Franklin thought. *I'm going to do it.*

"I want you to stay here," he told Scary. "Keep Pretty here, too." There was no way he was going to introduce his bizarre friends to his mom and dad this morning.

Scary raised an eyebrow.

"Don't worry. I'll lock the door, so she can't get out," Franklin whispered.

Scary flew over to Pretty's nest and formed a four-foot-high wall around her. He giggled.

"Wish me luck," Franklin said.

"*Gaglilee ikikizee,*" Scary answered. He popped his wings free and crossed them for good luck.

Franklin opened his bedroom door and poked his head out. He ducked into the bathroom, took a deep breath, and gazed at himself in the mirror. *I look horrible.* He was pasty white, with dark circles under his eyes, and his teeth looked a little jagged. There were a couple of lesions on his cheeks and chin. And a flap of skin on his forehead.

I look dead. I can't let them see me like this. He sniffed the air. *Or smell me like this.*

Very quietly, he turned on the water and dampened a washcloth. He tried to daub himself off, but eventually he gave up. He really needed a shower, but he didn't want them to hear the water.

He opened the medicine cabinet. There was his mom's deodorant. And his father's. And his own.

He took them all out and began rolling and spraying every inch of his body. He sniffed. He still smelled. He did it again.

And a third time.

And a fourth, until there was no more deodorant left.

I smell a little better. I think.

Then he opened the drawer beside the sink. His mother's jars and bottles of makeup were lined up in a row. He opened the nearest one. It was labeled NATURAL BEAUTY FOUNDATION SPF15. He got to work, sliding the goo over his face, taking extra care to cover up any signs of decomposition.

When he was finished, he examined himself in the mirror and shook his head. *Now I look like a dead guy with a tan. And I've used almost all my mom's makeup. She'll probably be really angry.*

He left the bathroom and went slowly downstairs—accent on slowly, because he was very nervous, and

because his left foot felt . . . loose.

Loose? Am I going to fall apart? This is so not fair!

He stood at the threshold of the dining room. There they were, his parents, at the light oak dining room table. His mom, with her curly auburn hair and a denim sundress, was buttering another piece of toast. His dark-haired dad, in his short-sleeved shirt and tie, was reading the *Daily Snicker* and sipping his coffee.

And then there was Sophie, his beloved dog, curled up beneath the table, gnawing on a rawhide bone. His heart swelled. He had missed them almost as much as he had missed Lilly.

Franklin opened his mouth to speak, mentally rehearsing one last time what he'd planned to say: *I know this is a shock, but I've come back from the grave. I'm still your son, and everything is going to be fine.*

But before he could get the words out, Sophie raised her head, saw him, barked wildly, and bounded toward him. She rose up on her hind legs and threw her front paws against his chest, pushing him to the floor.

She tried to lick his face and he laughed, saying, "No, Sophie, down, Sophie."

"Franklin!" his mom cried. She leaped to her feet so fast her chair fell backward. "Oh my God!"

"Son!" Mr. Ripp shouted, racing toward him, too.

His parents gathered him up in a group hug while Sophie danced around them in a circle. If he had still needed to breathe, he would have suffocated.

"Oh, honey," Mrs. Ripp said. She looked very confused. "We—we thought you were dead."

"Well, er . . ." Franklin looked from his dad to his mom to his dad again as they let go of him and took a step backward. "I'm not anymore."

"Oh, but . . . oh. That's wonderful," Mrs. Ripp said. "I'll go make you some eggs."

That's it? Franklin thought. *"I'll go make you some eggs"?*

At least his father showed some emotion. "It's . . . you . . . how amazing," he said. "I-I didn't know it could happen."

Please let me remind you that this was the way Franklin had grown up—participating in roundabout conversations designed to avoid asking questions. Remember, people who asked questions in Snickering Willows went away. Myself, I find it most ironic that Franklin "went away" because he did *not* ask a question. The world can be an odd place.

In the Afterlife, Franklin had met many dead people. None of them were from Snickering Willows, and they all felt free as birds to ask any question whatsoever that popped into their heads. Now that he was back, he realized what a truly strange town he had lived in, and what bizarre ways of behaving—and thinking—had been forced upon him and his fellow Snickering Willowites.

But he also realized that not asking questions was the way of things in the place of his birth, and if he wanted to fit in, he would have to go back to accepting things as they were—including parents who did not ask him questions such as:

1. What's it like to die?

2. What's it like to come back?

3. Did you think of us while you were gone?

As his mother turned toward the kitchen, her eyes suddenly got huge. As if the truth had finally penetrated. She smacked her forehead with the palm of her hand.

"I'm just crazy!" she cried.

"I know this is a shock," Franklin began. "But I—"

Rolling her eyes, she shook her head. "There's no time for eggs! It's the first day of school. You'd better get dressed, honey, or you're going to be late!"

"I can't go to school looking like this, Mom," Franklin protested. "I'm a freak!"

"Don't be silly," she replied. She cocked her head, appraising him, and pulled something off his face. "You are a little . . . flaky . . . but everyone is going to be so glad

you're back that they won't even notice."

"Your mom's right, son," his dad said, coming up beside Mrs. Ripp and draping an arm across her shoulders. "You know, I remember when I was your age. I was sure people were looking at me, judging me. When I got older, I found out that everyone feels that way."

"No one else died last June," Franklin argued.

"Well, you're not dead now," Mr. Ripp said. "You're just . . ."

"Undead," Franklin filled in.

"Got it," his dad replied.

"And I didn't even get a summer vacation," he reminded them. "I should get at least one day off."

"There's always next summer," his mom said. Of course, she knew nothing about the deal he had made with the Afterlife Commission. If he didn't kiss Lilly, there'd never be another summer in the Land of the Living.

But it was no use arguing. Franklin pretended to eat his breakfast (he didn't have the plumbing, nor the need, for food anymore), sneaking it to Sophie, and went upstairs to change his clothes.

* * * *

Mr. Ripp drove Franklin to school, which was on his way to his job at the Mystery Meat factory. He was a supervisor in the Top Secret Ingredients department.

As his father pulled up to the curb in his supremely uncool minivan, Franklin anxiously clenched his fists and got ready to face his peers. And Lilly.

"You'll do fine," Mr. Ripp assured him.

"Sure, Dad," Franklin replied as he opened the car door. *But I'm not so sure of that. You guys love me, but this is school. School is very different from normal life.*

He got out, hefting his backpack, and stared at the busy morning crush at the school entrance. His stomach clenched. His throat tightened. Maybe if he just sort of sidled in, no one would notice him.

His dad drove away and Franklin started walking toward the school entrance. No one noticed him.

So far, so good.

Then Steve raced toward him from twenty feet away on his skateboard, wheels spinning as he wobbled from side to side, and waved his arms, partly in greeting, mostly for balance.

"Franklin! Yo, Ripp!" he bellowed, and all chance of sneaking in evaporated. Heads turned. He heard a few gasps.

Steve jerked to a stop in front of Franklin and kicked up his board. He stared at Franklin wide-eyed, his mouth hanging open.

"Dude, you . . . wha . . . how . . ."

Franklin saw that Steve was on the verge of asking a question. One of these, perhaps:

1. How'd you get back here?

2. What's it like to be undead?

3. Did you die because you went skateboarding without your helmet?

"Hi," Franklin said, to keep his friend out of trouble.

Steve's mouth stayed open as he blinked a few times. He swallowed hard and smiled at Franklin.

"You're back," he said finally, looking him up and down.

"Yeah. I am." Franklin tried to smile, but his face felt stiff from all the makeup. *At least I hope it's the makeup. What if my face is breaking out in lesions and oozing sores? What if there are maggots in my nose or worms in my eyeballs? What if I still smell?* "I got a second chance," he added.

"Oh. Wow." Steve nodded. "Cool. Wow. I wonder if we'll have any classes together."

"I don't know," Franklin said. "I didn't register for anything. On account of dying."

"That's *one* way to get out of math," Steve said, and they both grinned. "Hey, the dudes and I boarded all summer." He drew himself up proudly. "I am *this close* to doing a 50-50 off Daredevil Bridge. We've got a bet going. First guy to pull it off wins a hundred bucks."

That was a very dangerous skateboarding stunt. Daredevil Bridge spanned Dead Man's Creek, which was shallow, rock-infested, and said to contain crocodiles. Doing a 50-50 off anything required skills, but if you fell off the bridge and plummeted into the creek . . .

. . . well, you just might die.

Steve wasn't really at the level of attempting something so hard, but he had always pushed himself to keep up with the others. Peer pressure could be a life changer—for good or really, really bad.

"I'll get my board out," Franklin suggested, thinking that maybe he could steer the guys somewhere else.

"Sweet," Steve said.

They walked into school together. Lockers slammed as kids got ready for first period. Some kids smiled at Franklin. Others raised their eyebrows. But to his continual relief, they seemed to take his return in stride. No one revealed the slightest bit of curiosity . . . just like good Snickering Willowites.

It's really going to be okay, he thought. *Maybe I don't look as bad as I think I do. Maybe my dad was right.*

"We've got to get the band going again, too," Steve went on. His face fell. "And I guess I should tell you . . ."

But at just that moment, Principal Lugosi's office

door opened. The dour, bald man with heavy eyelids and saggy cheeks frowned at Franklin.

"Mr. Ripp, if you please."

Yikes. Go to the principal's office? I'd almost rather face the Afterlife Commission again.

"Later," Steve whispered to Franklin, giving him a thumbs-up. "Everything's good. Except . . ."

"Mr. Ripp," Mr. Lugosi snapped.

"Go on," Franklin said to Steve. "We'll catch up later."

Steve nodded and turned away. Franklin followed Mr. Lugosi back into his office. The first thing he saw were the backs of two cheap upholstered chairs, which were facing Mr. Lugosi's black metal desk. A strange growl rose from the one on the right.

Mr. Lugosi stepped behind his desk and pointed to the chair. Franklin crept around it and looked down.

Pretty was curled up in it, swinging her tentacles, and the growling was coming from her.

"You know the rules, Ripp," Mr. Lugosi said. "No pets at school, unless they're service animals." He scrutinized Franklin as he sat behind his desk. "As I understand it, your condition doesn't warrant a service animal." He grimaced at Pretty. "Besides, I'm fairly certain this dog has rabies. I need her off school premises immediately."

Around Pretty's neck was a pink rhinestone collar and shiny fire-hydrant-shaped dog tag. The collar had to be Scary, who must have copied the words off Franklin's gravestone, thinking they amounted to Franklin's full name.

"Prrrretty not . . . dogrrr," Pretty growled.

Apparently the principal didn't hear her. He opened up a file folder on his desk and started looking through it. "We'll discuss your class schedule once you've taken your dog to the vet."

"Yes, sir." Franklin reached down and took Pretty by the hand. "Come on, Pretty," he said.

"Grrr," Pretty replied as she slid off the seat and trundled after him.

"About your death," Mr. Lugosi said, tenting his fingers and leaning his chin on them. "I heard something about a pack of wild Chihuahuas . . ."

"No, sir," Franklin said quickly. "No Chihuahuas."

"Humph. I lost a bet," Mr. Lugosi muttered. "Well, run along." He looked back down at his papers.

Franklin walked out of the office, tugging Pretty along. In less than a minute, they were back outside.

"Dog?" Pretty shrieked. Then she wrapped her hands around the nearest object—a municipal mailbox—and ripped it out of the ground. With a roar, she tossed it

into the street. "Pretty not dog!"

"Well, you're just lucky he thought you were," Franklin retorted, looking around anxiously to see if anyone had witnessed her act of vandalism. "I *told* you to stay in my room! You could wind up on a dissection table in a government lab. Or in a circus. Or on national TV."

She batted her eyelashes at him. "Pretty on TV?"

He huffed. Pointed. "Pretty, go home. *Now.*"

She turned in the direction he pointed. Both sides of the street were lined with buildings. In the far distance, the Snickering Willows Mystery Meat factory belched smoke and steam.

Pretty's ponytails bounced. "Where?" she asked over her shoulder. "Home is where?"

He looked expectantly at Scary. Scary sadly shook his head.

"Wawa."

"Then let's go," Franklin said, sighing. "We're wasting time."

Time better spent getting back together with Lilly.

"Road trip!" Pretty screamed with delight, as she grabbed Franklin's hand and swung it back and forth.

"Gazeeeeee!" Scary added enthusiastically.

"Just hurry," Franklin begged them both. *I have a girl to kiss—as soon as possible!*

Chapter Five:
In Which Our Hero Is All Ears!

✳ ✳ ✳

Franklin walked Pretty and Scary home, snuck them into his room, and dashed back to school. He stuck to the shadows; he didn't get tired, and he didn't get winded.

This is cool! Maybe there are some bonus points to being undead. I can stay up all night playing video games and still go to school. If I got onto the football team, I could run the ball down the field and back again and back again.

I'm kind of like a superhero!

At least, he hoped that that was how Lilly would see him . . .

By the time he got back to school, lunch was half over. Since he knew that was where he would have the best chance of seeing Lilly, he skipped Mr. Lugosi's office and shot down the deserted main corridor, then loped across the quad to the cafeteria.

His face was tingling again. So were his ears. His hands trembled as he pushed open the cafeteria double doors and stepped inside the noisy chaos that was school lunchtime. A sign near the lunch line read NEW MYSTERY MEAT FLAVOR FOR A NEW SCHOOL YEAR! NEAPOLITAN NACHO DELIGHT! TRY IT TODAY!

He smelled the tangy odor, stronger even than his own. Colors flashed and danced around him as all the groups claimed their tables—geeks, normal smart kids, dorky smart kids, future dropouts, regular kids.

And, of course, the jock sector, ruled by star quarterback Brad Anderwater, who sat with some of the starting lineup. His tray was heaped with a double serving of Neapolitan Nacho Delight.

Brad had it all—girls thought he was good-looking, he was the team's MVP, he had lots of cool friends, and he had all the teachers wrapped around his little finger. He was a bully, too, as guys who had everything could often be.

Brad glared at Franklin from his place at the head of his table. The other jocks did the same.

"Man, it smells in here," Brad said loudly as he took a big bite of the new recipe. "Like something died."

Brad's friends snorted.

"Hey, Ripp. I heard you died from eating a whole box of laxatives. You thought they were candy bars," Brad said.

The jocks cracked up some more.

"Or maybe you fell in a vat of pizza dough at Rigortoni's. And then you freaked out and died. Because, man, do you look freaky. Freaky Franklin. Freekin' Franklin." Brad's laugh was mean. "That's what we'll call you. Freekin."

"Hey, Freekin," one of Brad's minions called. His name was Sam Sontgerath, and he'd spent every other afternoon last year in detention for hassling guys who were smaller and more timid than he. "We've got a pool on how you died." He reached into his back pocket and pulled out a wad of paper. It was an enormous chart that read:

FRANKLIN RIPP CAUSE OF DEATH

Underneath that was written:

1. Terminal dorkiness

2. LZR!

3. Forgot to breathe

4. Overdosed on zit medication

"I thought you died from listening to yourself play the guitar," Sam added, pointing to the fifth item on the list. You're going to make someone at school really rich when you tell us how it happened."

Brad's jock-minions laughed like it was *soooo* funny. Franklin's face burned, but he kept going toward the cheerleading table, which was the next table over. A huge glittery banner announcing the Nonspecific Winter Holiday Dance hung from the rafters. He didn't see Lilly with the cheerleaders. They saw him, though. Lilly's best friend, Deirdre, leaned over and whispered to one of the other girls. They both glanced back at Franklin and whispered some more, and giggled.

Then Brad stood up. So did a couple of the other jocks.

"I'm not kidding, Freekin. Get out of here," Brad said.

The cheerleaders' eyes got huge as they watched to see what Franklin would do next. Other kids started looking over, too. Franklin could feel the vibe move through the cafeteria.

 53

As casually as he could, he hung a one-eighty. He was pissed. Embarrassed. He ticked his glance left, then right. No Lilly. No Steve, either. And a room brimming with kids who were staring at him.

And the morning started out so well, he thought glumly. *Trust a jerk like Brad to wreck my first day back. I'm glad Lilly isn't here to see this. But I'm sure the other girls will tell her all about it.*

He looked around for somewhere else to sit. But now the kids who had looked mildly surprised or actually happy to see him this morning looked away, especially if there was an empty seat at their table. It was as if Brad had said what everyone else was thinking: He was a freak.

He didn't see Steve or any of their old skateboard gang. Franklin had hoped they would show for lunch, to welcome him back. Lots of times last year, they'd snuck out at lunch to skateboard in the park. Maybe they were there now.

I have no one to sit with, Franklin thought.

Then Raven, the white-faced, kohl-eyed king of the goth table, stood up and made a little bow in Franklin's direction. His hair was black streaked with blue, and he had a lot of piercings. Everyone at the table had on white makeup and black-rimmed eyes. And black hair streaked with some other color. And black fingernails. And black clothes. Apparently, in their world, black was the new black.

All the goths were looking at Franklin. Seated beside Raven, a girl with violet streaks in her super-black hair shyly gestured him over.

Franklin hesitated. No normal kids ever sat with the goths. The goths were just too . . . uh, gothic. But the goths seemed to be the only kids willing to have him sit with them.

Franklin didn't know what else to do. So he headed on over. The rest of the cafeteria settled back down. *Nothing to see here, people. Go back to your Neapolitan Nacho Delight.*

The goths beamed at him. "Our table of death greets you," Raven intoned, softly snapping his fingers at two of his goth-minions, who produced an empty chair for Franklin directly across from him. "Sit; partake of the food of the wretched, ignorant masses."

He snapped his fingers again, and the girl with the violet streaks picked up her tray of Neapolitan Nacho Delight and offered it to Franklin like he was a god.

"Hi, I'm Shadesse," she said.

"Thanks, but I'm not really hungry. And I'm not dead," Franklin said. "I'm undead."

The goths drew in an awed breath and stared at him in utter fascination.

"Tell us of your journey in the land beyond the veil," Raven said. It was the first time anyone had shown the least bit of curiosity.

Trust the goths to live on the edge.

"It's kind of like here, only with more rotting," Franklin answered. But he wasn't interested in talking about himself. "Um, I'm looking for Lilly Weezbrock." He almost added, *Have you seen her?* But that would be a question, and questions were illegal.

"A mere mortal," Raven said disdainfully. "We're having a little gathering tonight, at my lair. To rid ourselves of the contamination of this monster house of conformity." He sighed and rolled his eyes. The other goths did the same.

"It's a party," Shadesse explained as she daintily loaded her fork with Neapolitan Nacho Delight and put it in her black-rimmed mouth. Her black fingernails had little white skulls painted on them.

And then . . . he saw her.

Lilly!

She was standing in the food line, chatting with a tall girl named Tish as they filed past the hairnet lady dishing out Neapolitan Nacho Delight. Lilly was as beautiful as ever, even just wearing jeans and a T-shirt. Her blond hair was hanging loose on her shoulders. Her sky blue eyes gleamed as she threw back her head and laughed at something Tish said.

"Later," he told Raven.

"It is always later than we think," Raven replied.

Eagerly, Franklin left the goths and worked his way through the cafeteria. His face tingled harder. His ears were getting hot.

He and Lilly were finally going to be reunited. He was nearly overcome with excitement. He could almost hear the sound track music for it, as if they were living out an amazing movie.

Tingling, his mind racing, he came closer. And closer. He smelled her heavenly vanilla perfume. He heard her musical laughter.

"So we're going to look for dresses at the mall," Lilly was saying to Tish as she selected a salad and put it on her tray. "You could come, too."

"That'd be great," Tish replied eagerly. "I'll have to check with my—"

"Hey," Franklin said. This was it. Here they were. He was one giant tingle. His ears were buzzing so loudly, he almost couldn't hear himself.

Tish stopped talking. She and Lilly turned to him

slowly. Waves of vanilla wafted toward him. Lilly blinked her sky blue eyes. Her shiny red lips parted.

"Um, hi," Lilly said as Tish looked on. Lilly's cheeks flushed dark red. Her smile was very small. "I heard you were back. You look . . . here you are."

Tish turned away as if to give them space.

"Yeah, I'm here," he answered. "Not dead and everything."

She swallowed and smiled a little brighter. Despite his nervousness, it made his ears tingle harder. They moved past the salads to the condiments section. "That's . . . that's great," she said.

"Yeah," he said. He cleared his throat. "Well, so . . ."

"Hey, Freekin, no cuts," the guy behind Lilly said.

He wanted to die. Well, not exactly, actually. But he didn't want Lilly to hear his hideous new nickname.

"Your parents must have been really glad to see you," Lilly continued. But her voice was kind of flat. And she seemed to spend a lot of time picking out a packet of salad dressing from all the identical packets of dressing, and choosing a bottle of water from among all the other identical bottles of water.

Franklin started to feel odd.

"Ah, I'll bet your summer at cheerleading camp was fun," he said, grasping at something, anything to keep the conversation going. He wanted to say, "It's still me. Still that guy you almost kissed." But he didn't. He was too afraid.

"Oh, yeah, it was a blast," she replied unenthusiastically. "Well, I have to go sit with the squad."

He looked over his shoulder. The whole cheerleader table was watching them. He turned his attention back to Lilly . . . at the same exact time that he felt something weird happening to his head.

To his right ear. It was getting . . . *loose.*

He swallowed down his shock and tried to act casual, hoping she wouldn't notice.

Then it kind of sprang off his head and dangled like an earring. He scrunched up his shoulder and laid his cheek on it, trying to look like he was scratching it. He snaked his hand along his jaw, fumbling for it. It fell off in his hand.

As he struggled to palm it, his left ear detached and splatted to the tile floor.

This can't be happening! This is a nightmare! I'm going to freak out right here . . . no, I can't. Not in front of Lilly . . .

"Oh my God," Lilly whispered, staring down at it. She covered her mouth. Then she brushed past him and dashed to the cheerleading table, where the other girls were shrieking and laughing.

"Freekin!" Brad called, as Franklin ducked down and grabbed his ears. "Freekin Ripp, nice ears!"

"Yo, Freekin!" Sam Sontgerath echoed. "You're falling apart!"

"Hey, Freekin, freaky dead boy, get your freak on!" someone else shouted.

The horrible nickname echoed all through the cafeteria. Franklin—*why fight it!?*—Freekin stuffed his ears in his pockets. Hopefully he could find some glue that bonds to skin when he gets home. He wheeled around and stomped toward the double doors. Rising from the goth table, Raven and Shadesse hurried across the cafeteria and caught up with him, striding along on either side of him like bodyguards.

"What fools these mortals be, that they would shun a traveler from beyond," Raven said disdainfully, jogging to keep up with him.

"Whatever," Freekin muttered, slamming outside.

"Come tonight to our gathering," Raven urged him, following him out into the brown, polluted sunlight. Wincing and shielding his eyes, he gestured back toward the cafeteria. "*She* will be there."

That stopped him short. "Lilly? At a goth thing?"

"At a goth thing," Raven confirmed.

"I'll be there, too," Shadesse said quietly.

He could almost hear Ms. Totenbone reminding him that he had one short school year to achieve the amazing life they'd taken him away from. One school year to kiss Lilly.

Lilly, who just ran shrieking from the sight of me. No, she didn't shriek. She just looked like she was going to vomit.

"She will be alone," Raven added. "No others of her kind will come to mock you."

No peer pressure? Just the two of us, the only regular kids at a goth party? Maybe if we can just sit and talk, and she sees that I'm still just me . . .

His mind raced. Should he go? Would he just make things worse?

How can things get any worse?

"I'll be there," Franklin told them.

Chapter Six:
In Which Our Hero's Hopes Are Dashed!
(And Then Glued Back Together!)

"Oh, please, party, please, please! Me love party!" Pretty begged Franklin as he changed into another pair of jeans and a long-sleeved, dark blue T-shirt. Pretty thought he looked adorable. She thought his shirt would look even cuter with a dead bunny head on it, like her jumper.

"*No,*" he said. "No way. Stay in my room. Don't let my

parents see you. Don't scare my dog. Just stay."

Then he *left*.

She couldn't believe it. She flopped down on his bed. Scary fluttered beside her.

"*Gazillikili,*" he said sadly.

Pretty dejectedly swung her tentacles, tangling and untangling them. Back in the Afterlife, they'd gone *everywhere* together, Pretty, Franklin, and Scary. She figured that when they came to the Land of the Living, it would be the same. But he kept leaving them behind.

"Me so bored," she told Scary. "Me so hungry. Pretty not want to stay."

"*Galakizizi zabibu.*"

"Franklin is not the daddy," she informed him, blinking all seven of her eyes. "So Pretty and Scary *can* go! Go to party!" She clapped her hands and hopped off the bed. "We go, Scary!"

"*Ziba,*" Scary said. He frowned and shook his head, fluttering his wings as fast as a vampire bat that had bitten a coffee drinker.

"Pretty and Scary do *not* get in trouble," she insisted. "C'mon, pretty-please?"

Pretty begged for so long and hard that eventually Scary gave in. But by then, Franklin had a big head start. She had no idea which way he'd gone. So Scary turned into a flying carpet, and they rose high above the towers and spires of Snickering Willows, searching for Franklin. They went to the school, which was dark. They zoomed around some more and eventually spotted a rambling brick building with a sign that read HORATIO SNICKERING MYSTERY MEAT FACTORY. The smoke from the chimneys made Pretty's eyes water.

"*Woodiwoodi,*" Scary murmured. He didn't like the factory. There was something freaky about it.

"Scary so afraid," Pretty said, patting him affectionately.

As they flew, Pretty trained all her eyes on the busy townscape below—so much to see, so much to investigate! Surely her Franklin was there *somewhere!*

After a few minutes, Scary soared over a large cluster of buildings crawling with people. Huge windows blazed with lights and bright, shiny objects.

"*Gazzebahalalawa?*" he suggested.

Pretty grabbed the edge of the carpet as she stared at the busy brilliance. Her eyes spun. Her heart pounded. "Scary," she breathed, "Pretty thinks that's the mall. Pretty thinks there are churros."

"*Zibu!*" Scary announced, rocketing toward the brightest, shiniest section of the buildings. A sign at the entrance read FOOD COURT.

"Wheeee!" Pretty shrieked.

———✳——✳——✳——✳———

Raven's very old, creepy-looking house sat at the very top of a very steep hill. Silhouetted by the full moon, Freekin stopped a couple of times to check his left foot, which still felt floppy. He worried it would fall off.

I really might fall apart. Maybe I can glue the loose parts. Or use some tape or something.

Incense permeated the gritty night as he reached the walkway to Raven's house. The porch stairs *creeeaked*. The skull-shaped doorbell clanged mournfully.

The front door squealed as Raven opened it. The goth almost looked happy to see Freekin.

"Good evening, returned one. Please, step across my threshold. I welcome your deathly presence."

Freekin followed Raven into the gloomy house. It was as dark as a tomb and just as musty. In the dim light, he saw the other goths, their white faces floating in the darkness like balloons. They were seated in a circle on the floor. He looked everywhere for Lilly, but she was nowhere to be found.

"Come. Imbue our rite with your mystical death energy and assist our communication with the great beyond."

A bunch of Scrabble letter tiles surrounded a

flickering black candle and a cone of burning incense.

"I don't know how to play this game," Freekin said.

"Please, it is a séance," Raven retorted as if, *duh*.

Freekin groaned silently. Or so he thought. In actuality, he had groaned aloud, and everyone turned to look at him.

"I sense unease," Raven said.

"Um, well, it's just . . . here's the thing," Freekin said. "Séances don't work. In fact, over . . . there, people kind of make fun of them."

Raven's goth-minions gasped as one.

"That cannot be so," Raven insisted, looking very shocked. "They who walk beyond have gone through the ultimate human experience: the passage from life to death. Surely they have much to tell those of us who have yet to cross over."

"Like you," Shadesse said, scratching her nose. "You can tell us."

Before I died, I thought the ultimate human experience would be kissing Lilly. Now I'm sure of it.

"Being dead is no big deal," Freekin said. "Trust me on this one."

The goths gasped again.

"Perhaps in *your* experience," Raven ventured. "We have attempted many times to contact John Lennon or

any of the Romantic poets. Surely they would have much to say."

Or maybe they just don't want to talk to you. Because you're goths, and you're weird, and you're kids.

"Yeah, well, maybe you're right," Freekin said. But he was ticked. *I should have known a goth party wouldn't be a regular, normal party. I hope Lilly shows up soon.*

✳ ✳ ✳

"Lilly!" Pretty screamed as she and Scary landed in the food court. Pretty recognized the human girl from all the pictures on Freekin's wall.

People scattered out of their way. A woman covered her Yorkshire terrier's eyes.

"Don't look, Fluffy!" she cried.

Across the court, in the picture windows of a large department store, silverware and goblets glimmered and gleamed on displays and shelves. And just beyond them, in a large clump, Lilly and some other girls rubbed lip gloss on their mouths and bronzer on their cheeks. They were weighed down with shopping bags.

Pretty sent an entire service for four crashing to the floor as she raced through the housewares department. Scary stopped to pick them up as Pretty trundled on, zooming up to Lilly.

"Lilly!" Pretty cried. "Hi!"

Lilly jerked. For a second, her eyes widened, and then she smiled a big, bright cheerleader smile. "Oh, hi. You must be that girl who had all the unfortunate plastic surgery." She held out a tube of lipstick. "We're trying on makeup to go with our dresses for the Nonspecific Winter Holiday Dance." She pointed to her shopping bag. "I'm wearing purple."

"Makeup!" Pretty grabbed the lipstick out of Lilly's hand and smeared it on her eyelids. She fluttered her lashes.

"Interesting look," Lilly said, and some of the other girls started laughing.

Pretty took a nibble off the end. "Mmm, tasty!" She popped the whole thing into her mouth and chewed. Then she grabbed another tube and swallowed it whole. And another. Leaping onto the makeup counter, she flicked open a black plastic container of eye shadows and began licking them.

The cheerleaders watched in shock. "Oh my God, you don't *eat* it!" Lilly said.

"You girls are causing a disturbance." It was a woman in a smock labeled *Highly Overpriced Products of Beauté*.

"Not us. It's that little freak," one of the other girls told her. "She's eating your makeup."

Pretty smiled, revealing zillions of tiny teeth coated

with a waxy rainbow of colors.

"Stop that!" the clerk cried. "You'll have to pay for all of that. Immediately!"

"Okie-dokie!" Pretty said. She leaned forward and plucked one of her little eyeballs out of its socket. She held it up to the woman. "Here!" Then she yanked out another. "Keep the change!"

Lilly, the woman, and all the other girls ran away screaming.

Utterly bewildered, Pretty watched them go.

Scary flew up with a serving spoon in his hand. He looked at the retreating throng. Then he turned to Pretty.

"*Galeeka?*" he asked, showing her the spoon.

"Silverware patterns later," Pretty said, cramming her eyeballs back into her head. "Franklin *now*."

Raven's party got worse.

The goths insisted on holding their séance anyway, and nothing happened. Bummed out, they put away their Scrabble letters and ate some black food—black olives, black crackers, black jelly beans—and listened to some really dreary music. Then they shared poetry they had written. Raven's poem was titled "Freezing to Death."

"Death is the snowfall,
Dead, dead, dead, dead, dead, dead, dead,
Hypothermia."

After a few more really depressing poems, Freekin yawned. He looked at the skull-shaped clock and realized he was going to have to leave soon. His parents had been so happy to hear that he'd been invited to a party that they'd let him go, even though it was a school night. But he had to be home early.

He nudged Raven. "I'm not seeing Lilly," he said.

"Oh." Raven got a funny look on his face. "Follow me, if you will, dark traveler."

They went outside and stood on the porch. Raven pulled out a pack of black licorice gum and offered Freekin a piece. Freekin shook his head.

The goth chomped his gum and glanced up at the moon. He was paler than any dead person Freekin had seen in the Afterlife, including Ms. Totenbone.

"Perhaps I exaggerated, just a little," Raven finally said. He fiddled with the gum pack, avoiding Freekin's gaze. "Perhaps she is not coming."

Freekin stared at him.

Raven took a breath. "For sure, she is not coming."

"You lied to me!" Freekin cried.

Raven gestured for him to lower his voice. "I beg of you, forgive me. I am the head goth of Snickering Willows, and you are like a rock star to us. I can't explain how much it meant that you came to my lair. Perhaps I can express it best in a poem—"

"I can't believe this."

Freekin stomped down the porch steps. His left foot was *really* loose, but he kept going.

"Please, come back," Raven called.

Without another word, Freekin started down the hill.

A rock star, huh? That part's not so bad . . . well, except who does that make me? Marilyn Manson or something? I think Lilly said once that she hated that guy . . .

He stomped on.

On the way home from Raven's party, Freekin passed the Snickering Willows Mall. He could hardly believe his eyes when he saw Lilly exiting the mall. What a major score, to see her again. She was so pretty. *Why* did his stupid ears have to fall off at lunch?

Just then, his ears started tingling again, and he cupped them with his hands.

Then Brad and his pack of jocks trotted up to the girls from an exit farther away. Brad waved at the girls. Lilly waved back.

She's so friendly with everybody. That's how we got together in the first place—in the library, when I dropped that book about the heroes of the NFL on her foot, and she got all excited because she's a football cheerleader and she loves football. And so I told her I was planning to try out for the team in the spring, which wasn't totally true, but she got all jazzed and so I decided to go for it and—

He watched, speechless, as Lilly—his Lilly!—glided up to Brad and laced her fingers with his.

Lilly is holding hands with Brad Anderwater!

"No," Freekin whispered from the shadows. He staggered to the left and grabbed onto a parking lot light. His mouth dropped open when Lilly gazed up at Brad with the same soft smile as when Freekin had almost kissed her last June.

"No, Lilly. No way," he whispered under his breath.

Then, in the glare of the fluorescent parking lot light, Brad handed Lilly a little bag. As the other girls and guys looked on, she reached inside and lifted out a little box. The girls all oohed and ahhed.

Brad opened the box for her. Lilly covered her mouth with her hands, then plucked up a shiny necklace. She threw her arms around Brad's neck and gazed up at him like *he* was a rock star.

No, don't do it. Don't, Freekin begged her.

She stood up on her tiptoes.

Wincing, he clenched his fists. His heart sank. He couldn't look away, but he couldn't stand to watch.

That smile . . . that gleam in her eyes . . .

Not Brad. Please don't kiss Brad.

She tipped back her head, just the way she had in the picture with Meaty Mouse, and parted her lips . . .

And Freekin had to look away. Had to *go* away.

He stumbled down the street in a daze. He forgot to stick to the shadows. He even forgot to look both ways before crossing, and he barely heard the screech of tires as he lurched across the street. He lost track of everything except the pain in his heart.

I was wrong, he thought. *I should have stayed dead. I should never have come back. I can't believe what I saw. I want to run screaming.*

He trudged into his house. His parents were in the living room, watching TV. Sophie trotted in from the kitchen, whining and wagging her tail.

"Hi, sweetie," Mrs. Ripp greeted him. "I hope the party was fun."

Freekin shrugged. "It was great." He faked a yawn. "I think I'll go on up to bed."

"It's been a long first day back," his dad ventured.

"Yeah." Freekin left them and trudged upstairs. He

stopped off on the way to his room to check himself out in the bathroom mirror.

Loser, he thought, leaning forward to gaze at his reflection. There were more lesions. *She's as good as dead to you. You'll never get her back. But how could she like* Brad? *Brad Anderwater of all people?*

Why not? He's everything I'm not.

Dejected, he moved on to his room.

"Surprise!" Pretty cried. Her entire face was slathered with lipstick, eye shadow, and mud. Tied snug beneath her chin, a party hat topped with one of her eyeballs sat between her ponytail ears.

Wearing a necklace of glow-in-the-dark chicken feet and a dead rose tucked jauntily behind one wing, Scary blew on a noisemaker.

Black banners decorated with spiderwebs and skulls stretched from one side of the room to the other. Crepe paper streamers and balloons stamped with IT'S A GIRL! and HAPPY RETIREMENT! hung from the ceiling. A row of shrunken heads wore tiny rhinestone tiaras. Headbands topped with bobbing bat jingle bells wrapped around gleaming human skulls. A poster tacked over his pictures of Lilly read WELCOME HOME, FRANKLIN!

"Party animals! Party down!" Pretty whirled in crazy circles.

"Where did you get all this stuff?" Freekin demanded, spreading wide his arms. *This is my second weird party of the night.*

"The mall! Pretty loves the mall!" she cried. She clapped her hands with excitement. "Makeup! Balloons! Churros!" She ran to a plastic Halloween platter decorated with cartoon skeletons. It was loaded with churros . . . and what appeared to be fried rats.

"But no skulls!" She shook her head with exasperation. "Scary flies Pretty back to the graveyard! We dig them all up, just for Franklin!"

Yikes! Those are real!

"*Gazu,*" Scary murmured.

Pretty showed him her filthy hands and cracked fingernails, then trundled over to the row of skulls and plucked one up. "Say, 'Hi, Franklin!'" She moved the jaw up and down. "Dig, dig, dig! Nothing too good for my Franklin! Party needs skulls! Dig up the graveyard! Pretty no quitter! Wheee!"

She tossed the skull in the air. Scary zoomed beneath it, caught it, and placed it back with the others. The little phantom zipped around in a circle and fluttered next to Freekin's cheek. Freekin finally realized it was his way of giving him a kiss.

Freekin felt his face crack as he grinned from ear

to ear. Those two sweet little weirdos had gone to a lot of work, just for him.

Pretty threw her arms around his waist. "No quitter! Not Pretty!" she sang.

I can at least try to get Lilly back, he thought. *I'm here, aren't I? What am I going to do, twiddle my thumbs until the end of the school year, and go back to the Afterlife—or somewhere worse—forever?*

No way!

"I'm no quitter, either," he told Pretty. He grabbed her hands. "Bring it on! Let's party!"

"Whee!" she cried.

And as he did a do-si-do with Scary and a swing-your-partner with Pretty, Freekin took a moment to acknowledge how lucky he was to have such good friends by his side for the biggest challenge of his existence.

Chapter Seven:

In Which Our Hero Attempts to Become More Like His Rival

* * *

After a couple of dances around his bedroom, Freekin heard his parents' TV turn off. "You're going to have to put the skulls back in the graveyard," he told Pretty as he frantically started taking down the decorations.

"Yes, Franklin," she replied, moving the jaw of the skull she was holding as if it were a ventriloquist's dummy.

He chuckled. "Call me Freekin," he said. "It's my new nickname." *I'm just going to go with it, and pretend it doesn't bother me. Then maybe everybody at school will get bored and move on.*

"Freekin," she said. "Pretty loves. Nice name."

"You'd think so," he replied, still smiling.

Okay, on to "Operation: Get Back Lilly."

He sat down and made a chart like the one Sam Sontgerath had pulled out of his pocket. First he dated it: *September 8–June 13.*

It read:

HOW TO BE MORE LIKE BRAD (SO I CAN GET LILLY BACK)

1. Coolness—band with Steve

2. Buy presents—need money

3. Looks—stop rotting

4. Jock—make the football team

Pretty bent around his elbow to study the chart. "Lilly," she said softly. "Kissy-kissy."

"Yeah. One can hope."

"Hope," she said, her voice dropping even lower. Her eyes drooped, her tentacles swayed, and she yawned.

He gave her ponytail ear a pull. "Go to bed, Pretty. You must be tired. You worked really hard on my party."

She smiled at him. "Pretty not sleepy."

Still, the little monster curled up in her nest and fell

asleep almost immediately. Her snore was like a gurgle. Scary soon joined her, cuddled up beneath her arm.

Freekin's mind raced as he studied his list.

He realized the football team was out, because tryouts were on the day he died. *Maybe I can become a total football expert. Read up on it, watch all the games* . . . As far as presents went, he realized that Brad probably had wads of cash. Guys like him usually did.

He thought about getting a job and wondered what kind. Then he had it. Under *Job*, he wrote, *mowing lawns, babysitting*, and *dog walking*.

By dawn, he had created a poster and printed out three dozen copies. He, Pretty, and Scary tiptoed outside to tape them up around the neighborhood.

The passing paperboy flung a newspaper toward the Ripps' porch as he rode past on his bicycle, beaning Freekin on the forehead and tipping his chin straight up.

"Freekin Ripp!" the kid yelled as Freekin grabbed his head and reset it on his neck. "Dead boy! You stink!"

"Grrrr," Pretty growled, and took off after him. Scary morphed into a Humvee and scooped her up into the driver's seat. It roared down the street like a hundred packs of wild Chihuahuas.

The kid glanced over his shoulder, screamed, and

pedaled as fast as he could while Pretty barreled after him, blasting Scary's horn.

"I'm sorry! I'm sorry!" the kid yelled. "I'll never do it again!"

He was right: He didn't. Pretty chased him until he rode to the newspaper office, threw down his cloth bag loaded with copies of the *Daily Snicker*, and shouted, "I quit!"

And that was how Freekin got his job as a paperboy.

＊ ＊ ＊ ＊

Freekin didn't have a bike for his paper route, so he used his skateboard. He couldn't find his helmet in his closet, so Scary morphed into one for him. Pretty balanced behind Freekin on the deck of the board, reaching into the official satchel labeled THE DAILY SNICKER slung over Freekin's shoulder and flinging the papers with abandon. It was a great system for the most part, except when she nearly took out the second story window of Freekin's next-door neighbor's house, and she knocked over the statue of Horatio Snickering III in Snickering Willows Municipal Park.

"Whoopsie-doopsie! Me so sorry," Pretty said. "Me go fix it." She hopped off the board and tottered onto the park grounds, just as Lilly crossed the street one block up.

Freekin nearly tumbled off his board.

Oh my God. What are the chances? Oh, wow, she looks so great.

Lilly was wearing a blue exercise outfit—long pants and a cropped sweatshirt that read SNICKERING WILLOWS CHEER. Her long hair shone in the rosy dawn. He felt the familiar tingle . . . but this time he was wearing his sweatshirt hood under his Scary-helmet. His ears *couldn't* fall off!

He took a deep breath. Part of him wanted to board up to her. Part of him didn't want her to see him at all.

I am not a quitter.

He pushed off hard and caught up to Lilly. He smelled her vanilla perfume, heard her practicing a cheer under her breath.

"Hey," he said.

She jerked. Then she looked at him and *smiled*. It wasn't a huge smile, but it was there.

"Hey," she said. She looked at the satchel of newspapers. Her eyebrows went up. She seemed impressed. "*Hey.* You have a job."

"Yup. I'm raking in the big bucks," he said.

"Cool." She nodded. "Big bucks are good."

Bling! He felt his ears loosen. But he knew she couldn't tell, because of his hood.

She absently toyed with her football charm. "I . . . I'm sorry that I freaked out in the caf . . ." She trailed off. "Um, I'm with Brad now, and . . ."

"I know," he said. *Does she have to rub it in?*

"I didn't know you were going to come back . . ." She dropped her hand to her side. "And your ears . . ." She grimaced. "I mean, I know it's not your fault . . ." She looked down at her shoes. "I have to go to cheerleading practice."

She blushed a little, and then she turned away and started walking again.

He couldn't stop looking at her as he pushed off, riding down the sidewalk. He watched her go around the corner, and even after she had disappeared, he still couldn't stop looking as he ollied off the curb and started across the street.

. . . and that was why he wasn't paying attention to the Snickering Willows Athletic Department sports van crossing the intersection.

WHAM! The front bumper slammed right into him. He jettisoned into the air and landed hard in the dirt. Scary morphed into his little phantom self, rolling head over end in the sky.

"Oh my God!" he heard someone scream. It was Coach Karloff, from the football team, who leaped out of the van and dropped to his knees beside Freekin. "I hope you're all right."

Freekin opened his eyes. "I'm okay," he said. He looked around for Pretty and Scary. Scary waved at him from the top of a phone pole. Oblivious, Pretty was singing to herself as she polished the brass statue of Horatio Snickering III with her tentacles.

The coach stared at him in disbelief. "You . . . you can't have survived that."

Freekin slowly sat up. "Maybe you haven't heard about me."

"Of course. You're Franklin Ripp." The man offered Freekin a hand up. "I remember you. You signed up to try out for the team. But you died before tryouts."

The coach gave him a once-over as Freekin got to his feet and wiped himself off.

"You're indestructible," Coach Karloff said.

A light bulb went on in Freekin's head. *Item number four on my big chart! Joining the team!*

"Yeah, guys can tackle me, but I can get right back up again. Like when you hit me."

"Let's just say we hit each other," the coach said quickly. "So there won't be any lawsuits."

"And I don't get tired," Freekin said excitedly. "I can run for eternity without getting winded. Seriously. I'm

like . . . like a machine! I could really be an asset to the team."

The coach thought a minute. "Huh. You might be right."

"I *am* right," he insisted. *Pleasepleasepleasepleaseplease!* "Give me a shot at trying out, coach!"

Coach Karloff scratched his nose thoughtfully. "The season's already started. I can't do that." He paused. "But then, I've never had a dead kid to work with."

He checked his watch. "Listen, I'm willing to give you a shot, but practice starts in an hour. You probably don't have time to make it, with your route and all."

"No! I so totally can!" Freekin couldn't stop nodding. "I'll be there."

"Okay, then." The coach scratched his nose again. "See you on the field in an hour."

"Thanks, coach. I'll be there early. I'll be there in twenty minutes."

"An hour's fine, Ripp," the coach said, with a wry grin. "I won't be there till six myself."

"Okay. Thank you. Thank you!"

"It's just a tryout," the coach reminded him. Then he climbed back into his truck and drove away.

"Yes!" Freekin cried, leaping into the air. Scary zoomed around Freekin's head, chattering excitedly.

"Zibugazeeba! Galilikili!"

This was *perfect*! This was huge! He wanted to run down the street, find Lilly, and tell her. But that would not be cool. And Freekin Ripp was all about cool. At least from this point going forward, anyway.

"Yay!" he shrieked, and did a happy dance.

Pretty looked up from polishing the statue.

"What up, Freekin?" she called.

"Leekadeeka!" Scary cried.

"Football! Football!" Pretty shrieked. Then she stopped. "What is football?"

"I'm going to be a football player!" he said. "A real, live player! Maybe. If I make it. I have to make it. I'll die if I don't make it.

"I have to stop saying that."

✳ ✳ ✳

Franklin finished his route, got home, showered, and redid the makeup and deodorant. He changed into black sweatpants and a black sweatshirt—holdovers from last Halloween—and grimaced at his reflection.

He didn't want to wake up his parents to give him a ride to practice—in part because he hadn't even told them about it—so Scary morphed into a bicycle. Pretty insisted on coming, too, and he figured she'd show up anyway, so he brought her.

"Behave," he begged her.

"Me so good," Pretty promised him.

They reached the field with three minutes to spare. Pretty climbed up to the topmost row of the bleachers. Scary sat on her head, morphing into a hooded sweatshirt, to conceal himself and Pretty from the eyes of the living.

Freekin hurried onto the practice field. The other guys were showing up in gray sweat suits with their names stitched on the fronts of their hoodies. Coach Karloff stood among them with a clipboard, marking each one as present when he called out their names.

Freekin took a mental snapshot of the moment. The grass sparkled with early morning dew. Crows were hopping around, snagging earthworms. In the distance, the Snickering Willows Mystery Meat factory polluted the horizon.

What a great day to be undead!

Then Brad strode onto the field wearing pads and a helmet, and he looked like he was about seven feet tall.

"Freekin, you're here," Brad said, disgusted.

Coach Karloff blew his whistle. Everyone turned and looked at him.

"This is Franklin Ripp. I'm looking to add him to the roster. Running back."

"Freekin!" Brad cried. "Not on my team!"

"Watch your mouth," Coach Karloff snapped. "This is *my* team, and don't you forget it."

Brad's face went purple with fury. Then he turned his back and stomped away.

The coach blew his whistle again. "Okay, let's see what our rookie can do. Ripp!" He walked over to the equipment bins. "You'll need a helmet."

Freekin heard a second high-pitched whistle. He glanced around, and saw Pretty peeking from behind the bleachers. She pointed at the warm-up bench, where a shiny black helmet sat gleaming in the sun. The "helmet" opened one eye and winked at Freekin. It was Scary.

"I've got my own helmet," Freekin told the coach. He wasn't exactly sure what his Underworldly friends had in mind, but he trusted it was good. "Thanks," he whispered as he picked Scary up.

"*Gazzeee,*" Scary whispered back.

"Okay, listen up," the coach said. "We're going to scrimmage. There'll be two teams. We'll start with a simple pass from the quarterback to Freekin. The other team will be after you, so stay on your toes. We'll see what you've got."

The coach blew the whistle and Freekin put the helmet on and assumed the position just behind Brad.

"I'd just start running now if I were you, Freekazoid," Brad muttered.

Freekin swallowed. *Don't let him get to you,* he told himself.

"Wahwah," Scary whispered.

"Seven, eleven, double-o seven, hike!" Brad called. Then he rammed the ball at Freekin, slamming it into his stomach. Freekin wasn't fazed at all. He started to run. He dodged the oncoming player, and the next guy. And the next guy. He was a bullet!

"Run, run, run!" Pretty shrieked from the sidelines. "Kill bad boys! Eat bad boys' eyeballs!"

Then the fourth guy creamed him and pushed him hard against the ground. A fifth guy leaped on top of the fourth guy.

Wham, crash, oof! Before Freekin knew it, he was buried beneath bodies. Then *more* bodies crashed down on him. It would have flattened a normal guy. Or at least broken something. But he really was indestructible!

"Kazika?" Scary whispered.

"I'm okay," Freekin whispered back.

The players unpiled, and Freekin got to his feet.

Pretty threw back her head. "Yay!" she cried. "Freekin not dead!"

"Okay, Ripp, that was impressive." The coach

scratched his nose as he consulted his clipboard. He made a few notations. "I'm putting you on the team. This Friday's our big game against Snorting Cypresses."

"Yes!" Freekin shouted, as Scary secretly giggled and kissed the crown of his head. "Thanks, coach!"

"AIEEEEEE!" Pretty screamed with joy.

"Over my dead body!" Brad yelled, unfastening his chin strap, ripping off his helmet, and slamming it to the ground.

"No, Anderwater, over *his* dead body," Coach Karloff replied. "Watch it or I'll bench you. Now hit the showers, all of you."

Brad glared at Freekin and stomped away. The coach patted Freekin on the arm.

"Good job out there. Just one thing—next time, leave your, um, little sister or your dog or whatever that is at home."

"Yessir." Freekin nodded, glancing over to see if Pretty had heard. But she was lost in oblivion, bouncing all over the grass like a crazed pogo stick.

Freekin moved his gaze past Pretty. His ears tingled. Lilly and the other cheerleaders had shown up at some point during the scrimmage. They were stretching from side to side in front of the statue of Mighty Meat, the school mascot, and Lilly was doing splits.

Wow, she's so limber, he thought, staring longingly at her.

She raised her hand and waved.

He almost raised his hand to wave back, then thought the better of it. Lilly had to be waving at someone else. Brad, most likely.

But when Freekin turned around, he saw that Brad had already crossed the field, heading for the showers.

Could she possibly have been waving at me?! he wondered, squelching his impulse to bounce all over the field like a crazed pogo stick himself.

Chapter Eight:

In Which Our Hero Encounters Some Non-Carnivorous Mystery

* * * *

The morning at school flew by. Freekin forgot all his worries. He was on the football team!

When lunchtime arrived, he thought about wandering over to the jock table, or at least saying hi to Lilly. But one look from Brad and he figured that would be pushing things too far.

So he left the cafeteria and went out to the quad.

Indian summer had come to Snickering Willows, and some of the kids were eating outside. A few waved at him. He waved back.

Then Steve showed up, his hands in his pockets.

"Hey, man," he said. "I'm sorry I didn't hang out with you at lunch on your first day back—I snuck out to go boarding with the guys. And I probably should have told you about Brad and Lilly."

"No worries," Freekin assured him, even though, to be honest, it hadn't been cool at all yesterday. But today was a completely different day.

Now, Gentle Reader, before I report the next utterance from dear Freekin, allow me to offer a gentle reminder. In a land with no questions, people are sometimes forced to state their accomplishments unprovoked. Resulting in what could seem like impolite self-promotion, rather than harmless relaying of information for the purpose of forwarding conversation. What follows below is the portrayal of one such occurrence:

(I'm sorry for the interruption, but I wouldn't want you to think ill of Freekin. As you may have already observed, I've grown quite fond of him.)

"I made the football team!" Freekin said. (Remember, information, not self-promotion.)

"Way to go, dude!" said Steve as he high-fived Freekin.

Their palms briefly stuck together, but Steve didn't seem to notice. "Especially since you missed tryouts."

I got hit by a truck, Freekin thought. "Asked the coach to give me a shot," he said. "And he liked what he saw."

"That rocks." Steve brightened. "I'm totally going to nail that 50-50 on Daredevil Bridge."

Freekin felt his stomach flip. "Be careful, Steve. That's a really dangerous stunt."

"Sweet," Steve replied, but there was a question in his eyes. Freekin sensed Steve was wondering if that was how he had died. Then two shadows stretched across Freekin and Steve. It was Raven and Shadesse. Raven was holding a large black umbrella and Shadesse was holding her hand in front of her face. Correction: in front of her nose.

It was on the tip of Freekin's tongue to ask her what was wrong, but he remembered to rein in his curiosity.

"Hi, Raven. Hey, Shadesse."

"I dink I'm allergic to domething," she said in a very stuffed-up voice. "My dose is very dwollen."

"I would guess it's sunlight," Raven said. He squinted up at the sky. "It causes so much skin damage. She won't let you see it, but her nose has doubled in size."

"*Raven.*" Frowning, she elbowed him in the ribs. "You daid you wouldn't tell!"

"I am sorry, Shadesse." He bowed his head, then turned his attention back to Freekin. "I wanted to apologize again about my . . . short guest list at our gathering, dark traveler. And also, to congratulate you on your acceptance onto the football team. You are like a gladiator, about to face the arena of trial by combat."

"Thanks," Freekin replied. He looked at Shadesse, who was blowing her nose on a black silk handkerchief. Her forehead was mottled with red dots.

"I think you're getting a rash," he told her. "Maybe you should go to the nurse."

She hiccuped. Her hand bobbed away from her nose, giving Freekin a clear view. It was as big as a doorknob!

"A good idea. I'll take you," Raven told Shadesse.

"Dater," Shadesse said to Freekin.

"It's always later than we think," Raven cut in.

The two goths walked away beneath their protective umbrella.

"That's some nose. She looks like Rudolph the Red-Nosed Reindeer. It's probably from all that incense they burn," Steve said.

"Maybe. The nurse will give her something to fix it."

"Hey, let's get the band going again," Steve suggested. "Let's practice this afternoon."

"Okay." Freekin smiled.

Freekin and Steve jammed for an hour in Steve's garage. As they tried out Freekin's new song, "Cheerleading Queen," Freekin had a fantasy of Lilly and the rest of the squad dancing to it during halftime at a big game.

"Um, Freekin," Steve said, staring down in horror at Freekin's hands.

Oh my God!

One of Freekin's fingers had broken off! It was tangled up in the strings of his guitar.

"Thanks," he said casually, trying to mask his embarrassment. He snaked his finger through the guitar strings and stuck it in his pocket. "Guess this is a good place to stop. I have to go home anyway."

Freekin skateboarded home. He found some Wacky Glue in the garage and glued his finger back on. It worked great. So he daubed some on his left ankle, too.

A little while later, he sat down to dinner with his parents.

"I'm on the football team! I got to try out today and I made it."

His mother's mouth dropped open. "Football can be so dangerous," she began.

"Hey, Mom, I already died," he reminded her. "I think I can handle it." Under the table, he moved his left foot up and down. It wasn't loose anymore. Sophie nosed it and Freekin gave her a little rub.

"I guess it's all right," Mrs. Ripp said. She looked at Mr. Ripp.

"I think he'll do fine," Freekin's dad said.

"Sweet," Freekin said. "Thanks, guys. We play our rivals this Friday."

"Snorting Cypresses . . ." his father started. "Just remember, they're not called the Body Snatchers for nothing. They take the worst students from all the other schools—the ones who have been held back two or three times—so they're bigger and older than any other team. Then they keep flunking them."

"That's what they tell me," Freekin agreed.

"Some things never change. And some do." Freekin's dad ate a healthy forkful of Neapolitan Nacho Delight. "This is the best flavor yet." He looked very proud. After all, he was an employee of Snickering Mystery Meat.

"Yeah, it's great." Freekin still hadn't told his parents that he didn't need to eat. His mom was so into cooking that he didn't want to hurt her feelings. So he took some forkfuls and spit them out when no one was looking. Then he palmed some of it and lowered it down to Sophie, who happily gobbled it all up.

"It's wonderful, dear," Mrs. Ripp said. She gave

Mr. Ripp a sly look. "Maybe you can tell us what's in it."

"Over my dead body," he replied. Then he made a face. "Sorry, son. I didn't mean to sound insensitive."

"It's okay, Dad. I'm not dead anymore." *But I might die again if I have to hear that joke one more time.*

After dinner, Freekin went upstairs to his room. Pretty and Scary were just returning from the graveyard. They had been there to return the skulls.

They had also been to the mall, to buy churros to celebrate his new acceptance onto the football team. (With Freekin's money, of course. It's the thought that counts, Dear Reader—don't you think?)

Freekin and Scary each took a churro. Pretty had six.

"Pretty and Scary go to graveyard. Pretty sees coffin," she said between bites. "Knock-knock, who is there? Pretty looks in. No dead boy!"

Puzzled, Freekin frowned. "You mean, there was a coffin in the ground, but nobody in it?"

"No body," Pretty confirmed.

"Gazikili," Scary replied, nodding.

"Huh. It must have been very old. The corpse probably rotted away to dust," Freekin suggested. He glanced down at his finger. *I hope that doesn't happen to me until the next time I'm buried underground.*

"Okie-dokie. Pretty just wonders." She sat on the edge of his bed and swung her tentacles. "Freekin can play now?"

"Freekin has homework," he told her. "Lucky thing I don't need to sleep. I can stay up all night and still do my paper route in the morning. And then go to football practice." *Football practice*—he loved the sound of it.

"You so lucky," she agreed, stifling a yawn.

"You should go to sleep," he said. "You're tired."

She started to argue. Then she yawned again and trundled over to her little bed. Scary waved at Freekin, then slid under her arm and let out a sleepy sigh.

Freekin got out his chart. Two days back from the dead, and he had accomplished three of his objectives— the band, a job, and the football team. All that was left was buying Lilly a present. And then . . . a kiss?

It seemed almost impossible that it was so easy.

On the morning of the big game, Freekin collected the money from his customers on his paper route, and several of them gave him tips. He got over ten dollars, just for himself! During lunch, he went to the student store and bought a little stuffed bear dressed in a Snickering Willows football uniform.

It's perfect! Lilly will love it!

He kept it in his backpack until just before game time. He suited up as fast as he could. He didn't worry about pads the way the other players did, but he did check his "helmet"—which was Scary, of course. It was the little phantom's job to hold on tight and keep Freekin's ears stuck to his head. Freekin had poured a ton of Wacky Glue on them, but the last thing he wanted was for them to fall off in the middle of the action.

Then he hurried outside to where the cheerleaders were stretching and checking one another's makeup. He watched for a moment, entranced, as Lilly sprayed more glitter on her hair. His ears tingled.

"Remember to hold onto my ears," he told the little phantom.

"*Gazeeka,*" Scary replied, giving his ears a hug.

Here goes nothing.

His ears tingled even harder as he pulled the little bear from his warm-up jacket and held it between his hands.

Then Lilly turned her head and saw him. Her features softened, and her lips drew up in a little smile. Freekin's ears felt like caterpillars were crawling all over them. Scary hugged them tighter, as if he could tell. Then Freekin took a breath and walked toward her. *Twenty yards . . . ten yards . . . touchdown.*

"Hi, Lilly," he said. He held the bear out to her. "This is for good luck tonight."

"Ooh, how *sweet*," she said warmly. When she took it from him, some of the bear's fuzz stuck to his fingertips. Hastily, he put his hands in the pockets of his warm-up jacket. Luckily, Lilly didn't seem to notice; she was too busy examining her bear.

Freekin muffled a deep sigh of relief.

"This is *so* nice of you," she said. She took a deep breath. "And after I've been so awful to you."

"Not really," he said.

"Yes, really." She caught her lower lip between her teeth. Her eyes glittered. "Freekin . . ."

"Lilly . . ."

Is this it? Are we going to kiss?

She took a step closer . . .

Closer . . .

His ears jangled and tingled. Scary gripped them hard.

"Ripp!" Coach Karloff shouted. "Let's hustle!"

Freekin almost took a chance and kissed Lilly right then and there, except suddenly her eyes grew wide and she whipped around and fled back to the cheerleaders.

Freekin had a bad feeling, and when he looked

behind him, the feeling was confirmed. A huge shadow loomed beside Coach Karloff, then moved into the light streaming from the locker room.

It was Brad. His eyes were practically shooting fire, and his jaw was clenched.

"C'mon, Ripp, let's go," the coach said, leading the way back to the locker room.

Brad walked beside Freekin.

"You. Are. Finished," he murmured.

Chapter Nine:

In Which Our Hero Savors the Thrill of Victory!

On the way to the locker room, Brad slammed hard into Freekin's shoulder. Freekin lost his balance and stumbled to the left. The glue around his ankle cracked. *Great, just great. What if my foot falls off?*

He moved ahead of Brad and caught up with Coach Karloff.

"I'm going to put you in early and we're going to do

those fake passes, so the Body Snatchers will tackle you," the coach told him, unaware of what had just happened between his two players.

"Got it," Freekin said.

"They'll wear themselves out. Then, in the second half, Brad will pass to you for real, but they won't be expecting it. Because they'll think you're dead meat from all that punishment. But we know different." He smiled wryly. "You're undead meat."

"Right," Freekin said, wondering how much longer the dead jokes would continue. He also wondered if Brad would follow the plan—or somehow try to sabotage him.

Freekin tried to remain calm as the team assembled for their pre-game huddle, jogged onto the field, and burst through the large paper poster of a Body Snatcher held by Lilly and Deirdre.

"AIEEEEEEEE!" came a shriek from the stands. Figuring it for Pretty, Freekin waved in her direction.

"Hey, Freekin! Kick their butts!" That was Steve, who was sitting with Raven.

"Guys!" Freekin called, waving.

"Okay, let's go!" Coach Karloff bellowed.

The team took to the field, squaring off against the Body Snatchers, who were enormous. Each one had to weigh at least 250 pounds.

"Thirteen, thirteen, hike!" Brad shouted. He pretended to pass the ball to Freekin, but he gave it to Sam Sontgerath instead. Freekin started charging down the field.

The Body Snatchers were on him like blowflies on a corpse. *Wham, crash, slam*, player after player leaped on top of Freekin.

"AIEEEEEEE!" Pretty screamed again. "KILL BAD BOYS! EAT BAD BOYS' EYEBALLS!"

One by one, the players got back up. The last one gave Freekin a hand up, raising him off his feet. Uh-oh. As he had feared, his left foot was very loose.

I guess the glue wouldn't have held anyway.

Meanwhile, the Body Snatchers were dancing with glee . . . and Sam Sontgerath was limping off the field.

"Substitution!" Coach Karloff snapped his fingers at Brian Vernia, who came in for Sam. "Run it again."

They ran it again. Freekin was tackled again. This time, Brian Vernia got some yardage. But on the next play, the Body Snatchers put Brian out of commission, too.

They're just too big for us, Freekin thought.

He watched the Body Snatchers massacre his teammates. Snorting Cypresses scored a touchdown. Then another.

His foot was getting looser. And looser.

Freekin jogged over to the coach. "Let me run with it now," he pleaded.

"Not yet. Second half," the coach insisted.

I'm not sure I'll be able to run by then, he thought. But he knew better than to argue with the coach. Then the halftime gun went off, and the players jogged back into the locker room. Freekin took it easy to reduce the wear and tear on his ankle. The water boy handed out big sports bottles and Freekin put his against his lips, pretending to take a hefty swallow. He set it on a bench and was about to sit down beside it when Brad stalked in, looking angry. Freekin got up and moved as far away from Brad as possible.

"You guys are giving the game away," he snapped. He looked down, spotted Freekin's water bottle, grabbed it, and guzzled it down.

* * * *

Brad came up beside Freekin as the team hit the field for the second half. He was blowing his nose, which was really swollen. It was almost as big as Shadesse's.

"I'm dot passing do you," he said. "You try do run the ball down the field, I'll tackle you myself. You are dot scoring any points." He blew his nose again.

"We're behind," Freekin argued. "If I can score a touchdown, you should assist."

"I'd rather lose this game than let you dook good," Brad said. He narrowed his eyes. "Lilly dumped you, dead boy. Don't even dink about getting her back."

Freekin didn't respond, but part of him was thrilled. Brad was looking at him like competition. That could only be good. It meant that he saw Freekin as a genuine threat.

Coach Karloff made the signal for the ball to be passed to Freekin, and all the players nodded at him. Time for their secret weapon.

But Brad didn't follow the game plan. He faked a pass, but he kept the ball himself. As the team scrambled to protect Freekin, Brad waltzed down the center of the field with the ball clutched against his stomach. He made the first down. He made the second down. Then . . . touchdown!

"Go, Brad!" the cheerleaders chanted as Brad slammed the ball into the turf and bent over, sneezing hard. His nose was as big as a lightbulb, and as red as a stop sign.

Then the Body Snatchers roared back with a vengeance and yanked the ball away from Brad. They made another touchdown.

The next time Brad got the ball, he refused to pass to Freekin again, even though Freekin was wide open and ready to receive it. The Body Snatchers got two more touchdowns in the third quarter. And Freekin's foot was getting looser and looser.

Finally Coach Karloff pulled Brad out of play and yelled at him. Freekin couldn't hear him, but he noticed Brad scratching his nose and forehead. Then his nemesis doubled over and fell to his knees.

"Medic!" Coach Karloff yelled.

Without much fanfare, two guys carrying a stretcher raced onto the field, lifted Brad onto it, and raced away. Her hands covering her mouth, Lilly leaned over the stretcher as Brad was moved out of the stadium. Deirdre hugged her as she sidestepped along with the medics, her gaze fixed on Brad. But after that, the game resumed as if nothing had happened.

Jesse Greenfield, the second-string quarterback, took over and followed the coach's playbook, passing the ball straight to Freekin. Freekin started down the field—but much more slowly than usual. His left foot was about to come off.

"Oh, no," he groaned aloud.

"*Galieekiliki?*" Scary asked.

"I'm not going to make it," Freekin told the phantom. "It's my foot."

"*Gazu,*" Scary replied, patting his ears.

"Go, Freekin! Go, Freekin!" Lilly chanted, obviously unaware of his problem. The other cheerleaders took up the cheer. "Move that pigskin, oink, oink, oink!"

"I'm on him!" a huge Body Snatcher bellowed, throwing out his arms as he planted himself directly in Freekin's path.

Then Scary popped his face out of the center of Franklin's helmet—only it wasn't his face. It was a hideous demonic mask of glowing red googly eyes, a pointed snout, and enormous, blood-drenched fangs. Even though Freekin couldn't see what was going on atop his head, he finally understood why Scary wanted to be his helmet. It was clear from the Body Snatcher's reaction.

"Gah!" the Body Snatcher shouted, dodging out of Freekin's way.

The next Body Snatcher did the same. The third turned tail and ran offside.

Undefended, Freekin raced all the way to the end zone and slammed the ball into the turf.

"Go, Freekin!" the Carnivores screamed. Lilly leaped into the arms of the nearest cheerleaders and they hopped wildly up and down, shrieking with joy. "Go, Freekin, go!"

They ran the same play again, Freekin and Scary, terrifying the living daylights out of their opposition.

The Body Snatchers jumped out of his way, shaking and quaking. One big guy burst into tears.

The Body Snatcher coach was going crazy, stomping up and down and yelling at a referee. Then he signaled for a substitution and pointed at the bench.

While the Carnivores looked on, the tallest, biggest, meanest player Freekin had ever seen slowly got to his feet. He had probably flunked every grade at least three times.

The ground nearly shook as the guy took the field. His eyes bored into Freekin's as the two teams got into position, ready to resume play.

The ref blew the whistle.

Grim and determined, Jesse passed the ball to Freekin. The players formed a barrier between Freekin and the entire Body Snatchers defense, concentrating on the monster player.

Struggling with his foot, Freekin limped down the field. As the crowd urged him on, he picked up speed. His foot started flapping like a swim fin. The big hulking guy mowed down the Carnivore closest to him, practically grinding him beneath his cleats. Then the next guy. Then the next.

"Hustle it up!" Coach Karloff shouted at Freekin. "Run, Ripp, Run!"

"Run, Ripp, run!" the cheerleaders chanted. "Run, Ripp, run!"

"KILL THEM! KILL BAD BOYS!" Pretty screamed.

"Gazigazi," Scary whispered.

Franklin put on a burst of speed. But his foot was almost off! It flapped around his ankle like a big clown shoe.

No!

"Woodiwoodi," Scary shouted anxiously.

The Snorting Cypresses hulk tossed another Carnivore out of his way like a bag of feathers. Two more of Freekin's teammates went down.

By the thirty-yard line, Freekin was almost alone on the field.

He pushed harder. Bones crunched. Something snapped. He stumbled. The ball almost popped out of his death grip.

The crowd groaned. Drums beat. The Body Snatcher cheerleaders were dancing with glee.

"Go, Freekin, go!" It was Lilly. "You can do it!"

"AIIEEEEEEE! KILL BAD BOY! EAT HIS EYEBALLS!"

Freekin reached the twenty-yard line. The people in the stands shrieked and pounded their feet on the bleachers. Coach Karloff raced along the sideline, gesturing him on. Lilly was jumping up and down. Scary was gibbering. And Pretty?

She was coiled around the Body Snatchers' goal post and waving her arms over her head.

"Run, Freekin, run!" she cried. "Freekin very fast boy!"

I can do this, Freekin told himself.

He pushed again. He passed the ten-yard line. Ten yards! He was almost there!

Then, with only five yards to go, the Body Snatcher leaped at him and grabbed him around the waist. Freekin's legs buckled. Scary squealed and fluttered to the ground, as if to cushion Freekin's fall.

"Noooooo!" the Carnivores yelled.

"NOOOOOOOO!" Pretty shrieked.

Freekin joined them. *"Nooooo!"*

"Woodiwoodi," Scary whispered.

Freekin was going down hard. His knees hit first, and he heard a terrible *crack-crack*! His chest slammed into the turf and something ripped.

Then he felt something odd happening to his shoulders.

And the crowd went totally, absolutely berserk.

"No! No way!" the hulk yelled.

Pinned beneath the furious player, Freekin managed

to peer upward to the sky. It took him a second to realize what he was seeing.

His detached arms, still holding the ball, arced up, up, then fell to earth, landing in the end zone!

Touchdown!

The hulk lifted himself off Freekin. He grabbed up Freekin's leg and slammed it down. Then he picked up Freekin's head and flung it angrily over his own head. Body Snatchers, Carnivores, cheerleaders, and spectators were pouring onto the field.

The Body Snatchers' coach was yelling at the referee. The referee was paging through a rule book.

"Freekin! Freekin!" The chant tore through the stadium.

Freekin tried to get up. But there wasn't enough of him to manage it. His arms, legs, and head were scattered all over the field.

Someone gathered Freekin's legs. Someone else located his torso. Sam Sontgerath held Freekin's head high in the air as the jubilant victors carried Freekin's assorted body parts around the field. Lilly was doing cartwheels. Still masquerading as Freekin's helmet, Scary chattered softly to Freekin, occasionally kissing his ears.

"FREE-KIN! FREE-KIN!"

Then they put him back together like a toy and

carried him on their shoulders, parading him all over the stadium. Steve and Raven caught up with him. Steve pumped his arm—his own arm—and cried, "Woo, woo, woo!" Raven merely nodded, which was a big display of enthusiasm for a goth.

Pretty trundled alongside, throwing him kisses.

"You so touchdown! Kill bad boys! Tra la la!" she sang.

Lilly trotted over to him and smiled. Really smiled. The way she used to. She made the little bear wave its paw at him.

"You won the game for us! You're MVP," Lilly said.

Coach Karloff grinned up at him. "*Love* the helmet, Ripp. We'll have to order some for the whole team. Give me the website for the company. And next time, tell me about anything like that."

"Yes, sir."

"Everyone, hit the showers," the coach bellowed. "We'll debrief and pick Most Valuable Player for tonight. Then, team party at my house." He gave Freekin another wave and headed off the field.

"We'll catch you later," Steve and Raven said. Freekin wished he could invite them to the party, but it was for players and cheerleaders only.

I'm a player!

"I have to go check on Brad," Lilly said. "Maybe I'll see you at Coach's house later." She turned, then glanced over her shoulder at him. "Bet you get picked for MVP," she called out and walked away.

"Sa-weet!" Freekin shot straight up in the air. When he came back down to earth, his body fell to pieces again.

But he was way too happy to care.

Chapter Ten:
In Which Our Hero Steps Right In It

✳ ✳ ✳ ✳

As Lilly had predicted, Freekin was named Most Valuable Player of the game. It was the first time that season that the honor had not fallen to Brad. The guys celebrated by throwing the re-reassembled Freekin into a shower stall and turning the water on ice cold. He couldn't feel the cold . . . but he could feel the warm vibes from the jocks who used to ridicule him. Then they dressed in street clothes and headed over to Coach Karloff's for the party.

After a couple of private moments celebrating their best friend's triumph, Scary morphed into a limo and Pretty drove Freekin to the coach's party in style. They stayed well out of sight, and then a block away, Scary turned back into his little self. Freekin's equipment bag, containing his dirty uniform and warm-up jacket, sat on the ground beside him.

"I'm sorry you can't come with me," he told the two little Underworlders, and he realized it was true. He wished they could join him.

"Gagalazi," Scary said.

"Pretty waits. Scary waits," Pretty told him.

"Thanks, guys." He gave her ponytail ear a little tug. She giggled and threw her arms around him, giving him a tight hug. Scary fluttered against his cheek.

"We so happy, football boy," she said.

Me too. Everything is finally starting to come together.

Freekin ambled up to the front door. It was open. Music pounded as the other guys greeted Freekin with high-fives and socks on his arm. A lot of them were scratching their noses. So was Coach Karloff, who saw Freekin, gave him a hearty wave, and came over.

"Hey, glad you could join us," the coach said.

Yow. His nose had ballooned to an enormous size, just like Brad's and Shadesse's. And it was very red. He sneezed three times in a row. "This warb weather has brought on by allergies. Helb yourself, kid. There's soda and bizza."

"Thanks, coach," Freekin said, noting mottled red dots across the coach's forehead. *Can it be that Shadesse, Coach Karloff, and Brad all have the same kind of allergies?* He grabbed a can of cola and pretended to eat a slice of Mystery Meat-lovers pizza. There were Neapolitan Nacho Delight crackers, huge bowls of chips and salsa, and tons of water and sodas.

After about an hour, Lilly and Deirdre arrived. The other cheerleaders gathered around them, comforting Lilly, who was pale and drawn. Her glittery hair was mussed and her makeup was smudged, as if she had been crying. But she was still the prettiest girl in the room.

Oh, Lilly, did you cry like that over me? Freekin wondered, as his ears jangled and tingled. But those were questions, of course. Questions he didn't have the nerve to ask, and couldn't have anyway.

Lilly's big blue eyes widened when she caught sight of him. Murmuring something to Deirdre, she left her girlfriend's side and walked straight over to Freekin. He anxiously touched his right ear, making sure it was still in place, and then pretended to scratch the other one to check on it as well. So far, so good.

"Hey," she said.

"Hey." His ears seriously wanted to fall off. But he'd practically coated them with glue, and they weren't going anywhere. "You were at the hospital with Brad," he said, which was Freekin's Snickering Willows way of asking how Brad was.

"Oh my God, it's so weird," she said. "He's making this bizarre grunting sound. Kind of like a pig. And he can't stop!"

Good, Freekin thought. *I hope he chokes.*

"I hope he's better soon," he said.

"I'm amazed you can say that, after what he did on the field," she replied. Some color crept into her cheeks. "I know he was supposed to hand off the ball to you. But he kept it." She looked down. "It was very selfish of him." Her voice was barely a whisper.

Freekin didn't know what to say. He completely agreed with her, but he wasn't going to tell her that.

"I'll bet you're thirsty," he said.

She nodded, and they walked together toward the large coolers brimming with cans of soda and water bottles. Freekin fished through the ice for cream soda, her favorite. He popped the top and handed it to her.

"You remembered," she said.

"I remember everything," he replied.

A deep purple flush began at the base of Lilly's neck and swooshed up her face to her clear, smooth forehead.

"Yeah," she said softly. Then she cleared her throat. "I'm hoping there's some cheese pizza. I've become a vegetarian."

"That's new."

"I decided to do it last summer at cheerleading camp."

"A lot happened . . . over the summer." *Like me dying, and you getting together with Brad.*

Lilly gazed at him. "A lot has happened since."

She took a sip of soda. Then they walked together to the stacks of pizza boxes. She got a slice of cheese and nibbled daintily on the end.

Then Deirdre came over, holding up her cell phone. "It's Brad," she said. "He's still making those weird noises."

As Deirdre passed the phone to Lilly, Freekin could hear Brad on the other end. Brad sounded like he was laughing through his nose, the way people did when their mouths were closed and they couldn't stop themselves.

Freekin secretly wished Brad would keep making that noise until his head exploded.

Lilly took the phone, and Freekin backed off to give her space. Not that he wanted to. But it was the cool thing to do.

"Brad, try to take a breath. Calm down," she pleaded.

Freekin didn't want to look like he was eavesdropping, so he walked over to the open window, where Pretty and Scary were looking in. Scary fluttered his wings, and Pretty shook her head.

"Bad party," Pretty said. "No churros. No skulls."

"Your parties are better," Freekin assured her. She preened.

Freekin looked back at Lilly. She was still on the phone with Brad, and the cheerleaders had drifted around her. He gazed around the room. Looking a little bruised and battered, Sam Sontgerath smiled at him. Jesse Greenfield bobbed his head. It was hard to believe that less than a week ago, they were pretty much his complete and total enemies.

Lilly finally hung up. She ran her hands through her hair, gazed around, and walked back to Freekin. His ears felt wiggly.

She blushed. "Um, Deirdre's mom is going to drive me over to see Brad," she said. "They think he might be having a mental breakdown."

"Bummer," he said, trying to sound like he meant it.

"Okay." She took a breath. "So . . . thank you again for the bear."

Then she turned and walked out of the house. He waited for a while, wishing she would come back, and when she didn't, he decided it was time to go home. Freekin found Coach Karloff. "Thanks for putting me on the team," he said.

"You earned your spot," the coach replied. "MVP in your first game. Not too shabby, Ripp."

Freekin walked out of the house and down the stairs.

"Yo, Carnivore!" Brian Vernia shouted.

Then he, Sam, Jesse, and a whole bunch of the other guys dumped a huge punch bowl filled with ice water all over Freekin.

"Yow!" Freekin cried, although he couldn't feel the cold at all.

"*Now* you're a full-fledged Carnivore!" Brian yelled, and they all laughed and clapped him on the back.

"Thanks, guys, a whole bunch," he said, laughing.

"No problem. Anytime," Brian said, scratching his nose. Jesse sneezed. And Sam's forehead was red.

Oh my God. Can they all have allergies, too? What's going on?

The guys filed back into the house, and Pretty and Scary met Freekin around the side. Scary began to morph into a limo, but Freekin stopped him.

"Could you be a skateboard?" he asked. "I do my best thinking on my board."

"*Gazieloo,*" Scary replied. Then he morphed not into a skateboard, but a helmet.

Freekin shrugged. "It's probably okay if I don't wear a helmet tonight," he said. "I got totally dismembered before and I'm fine. Well, except for my left foot. I'll have to work on that."

Scary turned into a board. Freekin hoisted his equipment bag over his shoulder and stepped on. Pretty jumped on behind him.

"Heave ho, Freekin!" she cried.

He pushed off and began to ride through the fume-laden night air. The spires and chimneys of Snickering Willows Mystery Meat factory stood out like black paper cutouts before the bone white full moon. Riding along, he thought first about Lilly, replaying every moment they had spent together tonight. She had really liked the bear. Getting her a present had been a fantastic idea.

Then he thought about all the people who were getting bad colds, and Brad, who may actually have gone insane. Maybe it was from the stress of making sure Lilly still liked him better. The thought gave Freekin a little thrill.

The shortest route home meant crossing Daredevil Bridge, so he took a left at Last Gasp Avenue and pushed along, performing a few simple skateboarding tricks—some basic ollies and some grinds.

"Ooh, Freekin! You so tricky!" Pretty cried.

Then, as they neared the bridge, he heard the sound of another set of wheels, landing hard, followed by a grunt.

It was Steve, sprawled across the wooden walkway. It was obvious he had fallen off the rail and slammed down hard on his side. He was wearing jeans and a jacket—but no pads that Freekin could see, and no helmet.

Before Freekin could call out, Steve grabbed his board and climbed back onto the rail. He centered himself on the board and pushed off, balancing precariously on the narrow edge.

"Hey, Steve," Freekin said, trying not to startle him.

"Yo!" Steve held out his arms for balance. "Check it out! I'm going to win that hundred bucks!"

Freekin watched him teeter. One wobble too far to the right, and Steve was going to go over . . . right into Dead Man's Creek. With no helmet, in the dark.

"Steve," Freekin said anxiously, "stop."

Steve bent his knees and leaped up, then sailed the board down to the floor of the bridge. He fell off again, landing hard on his butt.

"You distracted me!" he accused Freekin. He winced a little as he dusted off his jeans and got back to his feet. He kicked up his board and began to hoist himself back up onto the rail. "I almost had it that time."

"Steve, stop. You didn't. Hey, man, think about what you're doing."

Steve frowned at him. "It should be obvious. I'm winning a bet."

I can't let him do this, Freekin thought. "This is dangerous. Really dangerous. Did you ever stop to think about what you were doing? Whether it was safe or not? Did it at least occur to you to ask some basic questions?"

Steve stared at him. "Freekin, I'm not hearing this right."

Freekin realized what he'd said. And he realized he'd been right to say it.

"Yes. Ask some questions. Because I should have, Steve. I wasn't sure what I was doing when I died, and I wanted to ask a question—it was on the tip of my tongue—and I didn't. And I died."

"You . . ." Steve's mouth dropped open. His eyes practically spun. He held his board against his chest and took a step away from Freekin. "Dude, you're talking about breaking the law."

Freekin held out his hands. "Steve, I'm talking about dying. I should have asked, 'Is this safe? Can I get hurt? What do I do if something goes wrong?' And I didn't. So I'm asking you. Out here, in the dark, with no backup, no helmet—is *this* safe?"

"I don't know you," Steve said. "What happened to you after you died?" He dropped his board and covered his mouth with both hands, shaking his head wildly.

"You made me do that! You made me ask you that!" Steve whisper-shouted. "And we're both lucky nobody was around to hear."

Then he turned and fled into the night.

"I'm glad I did it," Freekin said to Pretty and Scary, who nodded quietly in response. But he felt as if he were the one falling off the bridge into the shallow, pitch-black water. He had done the worst thing a person who lived in Snickering Willows could do.

He had asked a question.

Chapter Eleven:
In Which Curiosity Kills
No Cats

Dejected, Freekin got back onto Scary-the-skateboard and headed for home. Clouds rolled across the sky—or maybe they were plumes of pollution from the Mystery Meat factory. Experimentally, he touched his nose to see if it was getting swollen. He didn't feel any itchiness. He didn't know if he could. But his nose felt the same size as always.

Pretty clung to him on the back of the board. "Steve so dumbo, la la," she sang. "Eat Steve's brains, tra la la."

"*La la la,*" Scary sang.

"No, don't eat his brains," Freekin said miserably. "Even if he's not using them."

"Pretty no like the Land of the Living," Pretty said. "Too dumbo."

"It *is* dumb," Freekin agreed. "But it's the way we grew up—not asking questions. It's the way it is for everybody."

"Dumbo, dumbo," Pretty insisted.

Then the rolling clouds collided with one another and broke open. Rain poured down.

Freekin and Pretty got off Scary-the-skateboard so he could stretch himself into an umbrella.

"*Gazee, zibu,*" he announced.

"Thanks," Freekin said, even though he was still wet from getting drenched with ice water. Pretty huddled next to him. He opened up his equipment bag, took out his warm-up jacket, and draped it around her. It was so long on her that it looked like a dress.

"You so sweet," Pretty said, fluttered her lashes at him. She cocked her head at him, studying his down-turned face. "Sad Freekin, so sad."

"*Wahwah,*" Scary added.

It rained all the way home. The autumn leaves drooped from the tree branches like multicolored bats. Flashes of lightning bleached color from bushes and cars, reminding Freekin of the rows of headstones and tombs in Snickering Willows Cemetery.

When he got home, he sent Pretty and Scary to climb into his room by their usual route, while he went in through the front door. His mother was pacing in the living room. Her hair was wet and she was wearing a raincoat.

"Oh, Franklin, I'm so glad you're home," she said anxiously. "Your dad's gone out to look for Sophie. You know she's terrified of lightning. She got out and we've been looking for her for an hour!"

"Let's go look, too," he said.

Pretty and Scary were already in Freekin's room when he came in through the front door. Pretty heard the anxious voices downstairs and the two Underworlders tiptoed down the hall to the top of the stairs to listen.

"Uh-oh," Pretty told Scary. "Freekin so sad. Freekin loves dog. *Real* dog," she added under her breath. Then she brightened. "Pretty looks for Sophie! Scary looks for Sophie! Freekin is happy!"

"*Gazkeeka woodiwoodi,*" Scary said.

"Heave ho, Scary," she insisted. But he didn't budge.

Pretty huffed. She put her hands on her hips and shook her head at him. Then she trundled back over to the windowsill and pushed up the sash.

"Pretty goes," she announced, and out she slithered.

I must interject a moment here, I being your Narrator, of course. I would hate for you to think that Scary did not join in Pretty's search for Sophie. During most of this story, Scary has been plucky indeed. But the fact of the matter is that Scary is actually rather timid. The thunder and lightning were terrifying for him. Yet he hesitated only a moment, and summoned his courage to follow Pretty into the fierce storm.

However, in that moment of hesitation, he lost track of Pretty altogether. That did not stop him. He flew out the window into the downpour, calling for her. But the weather was so wild that she couldn't hear him.

And so, for the first time in this entire narrative, the two little creatures were separated. But I also want to make sure that you know that Scary did search for Sophie. He simply looked in places other than the ones where Pretty did.

I'm sorry for the interruption, but as I am quite fond of Scary, I didn't want you to think ill of him. I have a habit of getting attached to my subjects.

Thus it was that Pretty trundled through the rain all by herself. "Dog-dog-doggie!" she called. "Yoo hoo! Knock knock!"

She was unaware that as she moved across town, quite a large number of cats started following her, yowling and crying as if she were some long-lost relative. Maybe it was something in her tone of voice, or the way she smelled, or that they sensed her kindness, but they fell in love in with her.

She rolled past the school and through the bad part of town, and then, finally, to the very edge of town, where the sprawling hulk of the Snickering Willows Mystery Meat factory clanked and whirred, late on that fateful Friday night. She probably would have trundled right past the twisted gates, except that a long black car drove right up to them, and a man leaned out and spoke into a small rectangular speaker. "Dead men tell no tales."

To her astonishment, the man looked very much like Brad Anderwater, the bad boy who was so mean to Freekin. Only he was much older, and he looked even meaner, with heavy, dark eyebrows and a tight, angry face.

From what Pretty knew of the Land of the Living, she thought he might be Brad's daddy. And she was right. Ian Anderwater, father of Brad Anderwater, was the

Vice President and Chief Undertaking Officer of the Top Secret Ingredients department. And he was there for an emergency meeting of the highest officials of the company.

(Which meant that Freekin's dad was *not* there, as he was not a high official. He was only a supervisor, and he didn't even know there was an emergency. Besides, you may recall that he was out looking for Sophie. I am telling you all this because I, your Narrator, am very fond of Mr. Ripp as well, and would hate for you to think ill of him.)

There was a buzzing sound, followed by a hum as the twisted gates slowly opened. Seized with curiosity, Pretty glommed on to the bumper of Mr. Anderwater's long dark car as he drove through.

She didn't realize that the massive herd of cats was perplexed by the moving barrier, and they yowled and meowed as their beloved Pretty disappeared into the darkness.

The car rolled for a few feet across a vast expanse of blacktop, and then it entered a tunnel. Down, down it went, and for a few moments, Pretty wondered if Mr. Anderwater was driving to the Underworld.

But then they came out of the tunnel into an underground parking area brimming with cars. Mr.

Anderwater parked next to an empty car with a sign on the side that read CHIEF OF SNICKERING WILLOWS POLICE DEPARTMENT. And the car beside *that* one said OFFICE OF THE MAYOR, SNICKERING WILLOWS.

Mr. Anderwater got out and headed for a shiny metal door. He pointed something at it and it opened. It was an elevator.

Pretty thought about leaving then. She knew she couldn't go into the elevator with Mr. Anderwater. He would probably think, like everybody else, that she was a rabid dog and no doubt, rabid dogs got kicked out of the Mystery Meat factory.

But her curiosity had grown. She wanted to see where he was going, and she was curious about the factory. She didn't forget that she was searching for Sophie. In fact, she reasoned, Sophie might have snuck in here herself, to get out of the rain *and* get some free Mystery Meat.

As luck would have it, she spied a door on the right side of the elevator that had been left ajar. She saw stairs. She rolled across the empty parking area and started climbing them.

Up, up, up she struggled, thwacking her tentacles and pulling herself up, kind of like a hermit crab. Each time she reached another floor, she peeked her head out into the hall, to see if Mr. Anderwater had come out of the elevator. She went up thirteen flights, then thirteen more.

On the 113th floor, the elevator slid open, and Mr. Anderwater came out. Pretty peered around the door and watched him press his hand on the center of a glowing white door across a heavily carpeted hall. A sign on the door read ULTRA TOP SECRET INGREDIENTS ROOM. NO ADMITTANCE WITHOUT ULTRA TOP SECRET CLEARANCE.

The center of the door glowed red in a hand shape around Mr. Anderwater's fingers and thumb.

"Anderwater, Ian. Identification complete," a voice said. *"Enter."*

The door opened. As he started to cross the threshold, Pretty silently shot across the hall, came up behind him, and followed him in.

* * * *

Meanwhile, Freekin and Mrs. Ripp were searching everywhere for Sophie. So was Scary, in another part of town.

"Sophie! Sophie!" Freekin cried, as he and his mother searched the grounds of Snickering Willows Municipal Park. They wore bright yellow raincoats and hats, and Freekin held their navy blue umbrella.

"Sophie!" Mrs. Ripp cried.

But Sophie didn't come. Cold, wet, tired, and

defeated, Freekin's mom put her hands in the pockets of her rain slicker and shook her head.

"We may as well go home," she said with a sigh. "I'm so worried about her, Franklin. I think she got into something this afternoon. Her nose was all swollen and she kept sneezing. I already made an appointment at the vet's on Monday afternoon."

Freekin's brows shot up. "Her nose was swollen," he repeated. "She was sneezing."

Can it be possible that Sophie has allergies, too? People-style allergies? That's just too many allergies. Something strange is going on.

Pretty sees what? People are who? Pretty wondered, stopping at the top of a carpeted ramp as Mr. Anderwater strode down it. A dozen men and women in black business suits sat at a glossy circular table in a sort of sunken conference room. Large paintings of men hung on the wall. An elderly man was seated in a wheelchair beneath one that read HORATIO SNICKERING III, OUR BELOVED FOUNDER.

Before each person, there was an unopened can of Neapolitan Nacho Delight Mystery Meat.

"Anderwater, you're late," the elderly man snapped at him.

"Sorry, sir. It's my son. He's got it."

Some of the people shifted and sighed. A red-haired woman who reminded Pretty of Ms. Totenbone picked up her can of Neapolitan Nacho Delight, stared at it, and put it back down. She murmured something that Pretty couldn't hear. As quietly as possible, Pretty trundled partway down the ramp, cocking her head as the woman continued to speak.

Pretty still couldn't hear her. So she crept a little closer.

And that was when she lost her balance. The top-heavy little monster pitched forward and landed on her head, then rolled onto her side as her tentacles whooshed over her head. She rolled all the way down the ramp like a bowling ball and landed splat at the feet of the elderly gentleman.

"Hello," she said in a small voice.

"Anderwater, you know the rules!" the man said, glaring down at her. "Dogs are not allowed in here!"

Pretty sighed. She had expected this.

"Mr. Snickering, that is *not* my dog," Mr. Anderwater informed him. "I would never bring a dog in here, sir, and I certainly wouldn't own one that ugly."

"UGLY?" Pretty repeated. She couldn't believe her ears. She had taken a lot of abuse from these human beings, but everyone in the Underworld knew that Pretty was the most beautiful monster who had ever lived.

Overcome with fury, she raised herself up off the floor. "PRETTY NOT UGLY!" She grabbed a can of Neapolitan Nacho Delight off the table and hurled it at the portrait of Horatio Snickering III. The can ripped through his face and lodged in the wall.

The people at the table gasped and jumped to their feet. The woman who was closest lunged at her. Pretty stuck out her tongue, whirled around on her tentacles, and trundled up the ramp as fast as she could go.

"That dog speaks English. Don't let her go!" Mr. Snickering shouted. "She's heard too much! It's your job if she gets out of here alive, Anderwater!"

Bells clanged. An alarm siren wailed. Pretty started screaming and fire erupted from her eyes and mouth. Flames licked the walls, ceiling, and floor. The glowing white door thudded open and men in firefighter uniforms wrestling a water-gushing hose burst into the room.

"AIEEE!" Pretty cried, and she darted through their legs. She fled into the elevator, but she couldn't reach the buttons. She zoomed back out and took the stairs.

One, two, three . . . down 113 flights of stairs she huffed and panted.

She burst out of the door into the parking area . . . to find Mr. Anderwater barring her way. He was dressed like a fireman, crouched low, with his legs spread wide apart. He held a gun in one hand, and a protective shield in the other.

"Thought you'd get away," he sneered. "*I* took the elevator."

Her eyes spun. She darted left. So did he.

She darted right. So did he.

She opened her mouth and spewed flames at him, but his shield protected him.

"You. Are. Dead," he told her. "And once I find out who you're working for, they're dead, too."

Freekin not dead! she thought. *Scary not dead! No!*

She started to cry. As she sobbed, a loud, screeching howl echoed off the walls.

"Stop that!" he yelled at her.

But Pretty wasn't making any noise at all. She was weeping silently.

Another howl echoed through the large space. And another. And all Pretty's adoring cats came racing through the tunnel and into the parking area like a whooshing cat river. Who knows why they came at that precise moment? Did they have some kind of cat sense that their beloved Pretty was in trouble? Did they smell the odor of Mystery Meat cooking in the fire that Pretty had started?

Whatever the case, they galloped to her rescue like a herd of wild horses, not tabbies and American Shorthairs.

As they advanced, Mr. Anderwater whirled around and fired his gun. But his bullets went wild, and the cats kept coming. They swarmed around and over him as if he weren't even there, and knocked him over on his back.

"No, stop! NOOOOO!" he shouted. The hand with the gun raised upward; he got off one more shot; then he dropped the gun and his hand slowly sank in the stampede of fur and whiskers.

"Kitties!" Pretty cried. "Kitties come!" She rolled over to Mr. Anderwater, who had fainted dead away, fished in his pockets, and got his car keys. Then she barreled over to his long dark car, reached around the door handle, and yanked the entire door off its hinges. She tossed it behind her, which set off the car alarm in the Chief of Police's car.

While she hoisted herself behind the wheel and jammed the key in the ignition, the cats (including one Scary cat) swarmed in, yowling and jostling one another. Then Pretty gunned the engine and drove that car out

of there like the most beautiful monster in the entire Underworld in fear for her own life, and those of the ones she loved.

Chapter Twelve:
Twenty Questions
(Or, Perhaps, Four)

Freekin and his mom came home from their search for Sophie just as Mr. Ripp drove up the driveway. It was still pouring rain, and none of them had seen their pooch.

"I'll go back out in the car with you," Freekin told his dad when he entered the house.

"No, you stay home. Something's going around,"

Mr. Ripp said. "I drove by the hospital and the emergency room is jammed. People were sneezing and making disgusting noises."

"Kids have been getting sick like that at school," Freekin ventured. "It's allergies."

"Well, maybe being undead will help with that." His dad wiped his face with a handkerchief and rubbed his hands together to warm them. "I heard you won the game."

"Yes," Freekin said. "Let's talk about it later."

"Of course. Go on up to bed," his mom told him. "We'll let you know as soon as we find Sophie."

Freekin would have argued, except he knew that he, Pretty, and Scary could easily sneak back out the window to continue the search.

"Congrats on the win," his dad said.

He went upstairs. When he opened the door, he found Pretty and Scary seated on the floor, surrounded by at least two dozen wet, purring cats. A kitten sat on Pretty's head. Several others were batting at her tentacles.

"Hey, guys," Freekin said. "What's going on? What's with all these cats?"

"Pretty looks for Sophie," Pretty said. Her big eyes welled. Her other ones stared unblinking at him. "Yoo hoo! Puppy-pup! Kitties come. They love Pretty.

OWWWW!" She bared her teeth at a large tortoiseshell cat that had playfully nipped one of her tentacles. Oblivious, the cat batted her ponytail ear.

"Shh. We can't keep them," Freekin said as he shuffled a few pure black tomcats out of his path. "I guess you didn't find Sophie."

"No." She took a breath, gazed at Freekin with all her eyes, then exhaled. "Me see nothing. Me so sorry."

"What about you?" he asked Scary.

"*Wahwah,* Sophie," Scary said sadly.

You do understand why Pretty did not tell Freekin about what she had seen and heard at the Mystery Meat factory, do you not? Mr. Anderwater had threatened to harm anyone she told. So to protect him, and Scary, and by extension, Sophie and the Ripps, she sealed her lips. Which was difficult, given how many teeth she had.

It rained all day Saturday. Coach Karloff called Freekin to tell him that practice was canceled for the weekend not so much because of the weather, but because so many of the players were ill.

"Brad's still making that weird noise," he said.

And Sophie didn't come home.

There was big news: A freak fire had broken out at the Snickering Willows Mystery Meat factory, and

operations would be halted until repairs were made. The pictures on the news showed that a large section of the 113th floor had gone up in flames. Mr. Ian Anderwater had been taken to the hospital for injuries sustained while attempting to put them out.

Freekin had never fully connected that Brad's dad was his father's boss's boss at the factory. It kind of amazed him—and it made him all the more glad that Brad was sidelined. The Ripps didn't need the Anderwaters in their lives.

"Guess it's time to do some home repairs," Mr. Ripp said. "Since I won't be going in to work."

Every time the phone rang, Freekin jumped, hoping that it was someone who had found Sophie—or that it was Steve. He hadn't heard from his best friend since Friday night. Had Steve called the police to tell them that Freekin had asked a question? Would they come and take him away? He remembered how terrified he had been that the government would lock him up and study him. Would the Snickering Willows Police Department just lock him up, period?

Finally Monday rolled around, with no police visits and no calls from Steve. Mr. Ripp drove Freekin to school, and as his father pulled away from the curb, Freekin saw him scratching his nose.

Not Dad, too, he thought anxiously. *I have to find out what's happening.*

The halls were practically deserted. At least half the student body was absent. His footfalls echoed down the corridors.

He went to all his morning classes, but there was hardly anyone in them. Students with scratchy noses got sent to the nurse . . . and they never came back.

At lunch he spotted Lilly in the half-empty cafeteria. Deirdre and the other cheerleaders sat with her at their usual table. Sam, Jesse, Brian, and some of the starting lineup sprawled at the jock table. Brad's seat was empty.

Freekin gave them a wave and went straight over to Lilly.

"Hey," he said.

"Hey." She didn't smile as she got to her feet and walked away from the table. He followed, and they stopped beneath the banner for the Nonspecific Winter Holiday Dance.

"Steve came over to see me," she said in a low voice. "He seemed really upset, but he wouldn't tell me what was wrong. Only that it was something that had happened between the two of you."

"Uh, well, yeah," he said. So Steve hadn't told her. Maybe he hadn't told anyone. "We'll work it out."

"Well, I think he stayed out of school because of it," she went on.

"So he's not sick," Freekin said.

She shook her head. Even though Freekin was bummed that things had gotten so strained between Steve and him, he still stood behind his decision to question Steve. Steve was still his best friend, as far as he was concerned. Freekin had done what he'd done to save his life, and he would do it again.

"Also, they think they've figured out what's wrong with Brad," she said. She made a face as she moved her shoulders. "They think it might be a vitamin deficiency. Or . . . or something like that. But it's called Chronic Snickering Syndrome."

"What? Are you serious?" he blurted.

She covered her mouth, looking anxiously around to see if anyone else had heard him. "Oh my God, Freekin, you just . . . you . . ."

"Sorry." He wiped his face. "I didn't mean to say that."

"You . . . you *asked* . . ."

She took a step away, her eyes darting left and right.

"Lilly, questions are important. I died because I stopped myself from asking them," he said solemnly. Lilly

looked as if she were about to burst into tears. But that didn't stop Freekin from finishing his thought. "There are some things that need to be questioned."

"No. It's wrong," Lilly insisted, shaking her beautiful blond hair.

At that moment Raven walked into the cafeteria, with only half a dozen goth-minions in tow. His kohl-rimmed eyes glistened with tears.

"Shadesse is afflicted with Chronic Snickering Syndrome. She lies in bed going like this." He made amazing noises that, yes, *did* sound like someone snickering.

"No," Freekin breathed. He was so sorry for Raven, who looked so worried. And for Shadesse, who was snickering her life away.

"Please, help us," the goth-minion on Raven's left—Freekin thought he called himself Tuberculosis—said as he clenched his white hands together. His black nails had letters on them that spelled R-I-P-F-R-E-E-K-I-N.

Okay, that's it. I'm getting to the bottom of this. First I need to find Principal Lugosi.

Freekin turned to Lilly. Reaching for her hands, he laced them with his, hoping they wouldn't stick together. He stepped toward her, locking eyes with her.

"Things are very wrong in Snickering Willows," he

told her. "And someone has to find out why."

"Freekin, 'why' is a very bad word," Lilly murmured. "You shouldn't say it in school."

"I'm going to say it in more places than school," he replied honestly.

Raven looked on intently. "We are with you, dark traveler," he said. The goths nodded.

"Come on, then." He gazed at Lilly, who swallowed hard. "You stay out of this. I don't want to get you in trouble."

She nodded. "Please be careful."

Raven and the minions followed Freekin out of the cafeteria and across the quad. He strode down the main hall to Mr. Lugosi's door and knocked hard.

"Principal Lugosi!"

"Come in," Mr. Lugosi said.

"Wait here," Freekin told Raven and his minions.

"Take care, dark questing being," Raven replied.

"I will. Thanks," he replied, and went inside.

Mr. Lugosi was seated behind piles of student folders. He was on a cell phone, and his other phone was ringing.

"I'm busy, Mr. Ripp," he said. "Very, very busy. You may have noticed that we have a lot of absences. It's a terrible vitamin deficiency."

"What's really going on?" Freekin asked him.

Principal Lugosi gaped at him. Color rose in his cheeks as he hung up the phone. "I don't think I heard you correctly," he said slowly.

"There's more to it, right?" Freekin demanded. "It's a conspiracy! Do you know what's going on? Do you know what's causing this?"

The principal blinked once. Twice. On the third blink, he rose from behind the desk.

"*I knew it,*" Mr. Lugosi said triumphantly. "I knew there was something wrong with you the minute you came back. I could smell it on you. *You're* what everyone's allergic to. You're making everyone sick, just by being here."

Freekin was as stunned as if Mr. Lugosi had reached out and slapped him. What if it was true? What if he *was* making people sick? What if he picked up some horrible bug in the Afterlife that people in the Land of the Living couldn't tolerate? What if he was a carrier for the awful disease that was taking over Snickering Willows?

The thought had never even crossed his mind. *I was too worried about myself to take anyone else into consideration.*

The principal pointed a shaking finger at him. "Now you know what I think. And what I *know* is that you've broken the law, Ripp. No one, and I mean *no one*, asks questions in my school. You're expelled."

Freekin turned and rushed out of the office. Raven and the goths were waiting for him.

And so was Lilly. "I had to wait and see what happened," she said, looking pale and shaken.

"We heard," Raven said, including Lilly in his statement. He looked at Freekin. "It was brave of you to ask questions. We're right to idolize you."

"Go, Freekin," Tuberculosis said. The other goths nodded.

"He's calling the police. I'm a wanted man. If they try me and find me guilty . . ." He stared hard at Raven. "Well, you know what that means."

"Yes. You will leave again. Forever," Raven intoned. "They will send you away, and you will never return."

Not to Snickering Willows or to the Land of the Living.

Lilly bit her lower lip.

"Well, until that happens, I'm going to find out as much as I can," Freekin told him.

"We shall help," Raven said. The other goths nodded. "We'd better leave. The authorities may show up at any moment."

They raced out of the school as if Freekin's life depended on it. Which, in essence, it did. He had been back in the Land of the Living for only one week, and

it seemed as if his chances of staying for thirty-seven more—until the end of the school year—were very small indeed.

Chapter Thirteen:
In Which Our Hero Partially
(But Only Partially)
Solves The Mystery

✳ ✳ ✳

Freekin, Lilly, Raven, Tuberculosis, and the other goths melted into the shadows as they decided where to go first. Freekin really wanted to stop at home and check on his parents.

"But I don't want to make my mom and dad sick," he added dismally as they darted across one of the streets. Though the rain had stopped on Sunday, the town was

still dripping wet. The air was soaked with the smell of smoke and cooked Mystery Meat.

"Freekin, think," Raven said. "They're your parents. They live with you. If you were a carrier, they'd be chronically snickering by now."

"I guess." He slid a glance over at Lilly, who was pale and frightened, and looked more freaked out than ever before.

He scanned up the block to see if the coast was clear, wishing Pretty and Scary were with him. And he was worried about Sophie. How could so many awful things happen at once?

A black limo pulled up to the curb. Freekin and the others jumped back, and Freekin hid behind a mailbox very similar to the one Pretty had ripped out of the ground when Mr. Lugosi had called her a dog.

The tinted driver's window rolled down. Pretty was at the wheel, and she waved excitedly at Freekin.

"Hi, hi!" she called. "Freekin! Pretty finds Sophie!"

"*Gazeeli*," Scary added. Freekin wondered if his friends could ever imagine that the car they were looking at was actually a shape-shifting phantom.

"Heave ho, Freekin," Pretty said. "Beep beep!"

"Allow me," Tuberculosis said. He hurried to the passenger door and opened it with a flourish. Squatting down like commandos, Freekin led Lilly, Raven, and the others into the limo. Muddy and matted, Sophie jumped at him the moment he climbed inside and furiously began licking his face. As he laughed and hugged her, the others piled in, and Tuberculosis shut the door.

The limo took off.

Freekin scratched Sophie behind the ears. "Hey, girl, where have you been?"

"Oh, aren't you pretty," Lilly said.

"Me so Pretty!" Pretty cried.

"Hey, dude, if that's your sister driving the limo, she's kind of hot," Tuberculosis said.

Pretty drove the limo slowly toward the Ripp house. Limos weren't very common in Snickering Willows, so it was a good idea for everyone to lay low. But with everyone already seated, it wasn't the right time to ask Scary to morph into something else.

"Look! There's Steve!" Lilly cried.

Sure enough, Steve was riding his skateboard down the street, hands in his pockets. Pretty pulled over and Freekin rolled down his window.

"Oh my God," Steve said. His eyes twinkled as if he were really happy to see Freekin. He then looked furtively around before approaching the limo. "Freekin,

the police are at your house. Principal Lugosi called them. Something about you being a security risk. Your dad's been fired."

"Oh no!" Freekin said. He ran his hands through his hair. "That's crazy. I can't believe all this is happeni—" He broke off as Sophie started to make wild snorting noises.

"Something's wrong with Sophie," Steve said, trying to look in through the window.

"She's got Chronic Snickering Syndrome," Freekin said anxiously. "We need to do something!" *She must have just gotten it from licking my face*, he thought.

"Pretty can fix," Pretty announced.

"What?" Freekin cried. "All this time, you could have helped all the sick people?"

She shook her head. "Pretty knows magical spell. But not for people. We not have people in Underworld. We have monsters. And dogs. Two-headed dogs. Three-headed dogs. But Pretty think she knows to help one-headed dog, too."

Pretty changed course, heading for the cemetery. She explained in her own wacky way that it was best to perform spells at a cemetery. Close to where the spirits dwelled. "Or the mall," Pretty added. "Pretty likes mall."

"To the graveyard, Pretty," Freekin said sternly. "Now!" By then, the sun was going down. Shadows spread across the limo as Scary pulled up to the gates.

"I did this," Freekin muttered to himself as everyone joined hands and carried Sophie among the gravestones. She was snickering like crazy. "I am what's making everyone sick."

He glanced over at Lilly. Her head was bowed, and he couldn't see her expression. But he could only guess what awful things she had to be thinking about him now.

Then he bent down and grabbed Sophie's chin as she snickered and snorted. "Hang on, girl. Please hang on."

The wind whined through the trees like a wounded animal. The weeping angels on the tombs and crypts of Snickering Willows Cemetery looked like they were shivering in the cold. At Pretty's direction, Scary placed Sophie on Freekin's grave. Lilly stared wide-eyed at his headstone, as if it had just dawned on her that he really truly had come back from the dead.

Then she caught sight of Lilly.

"Freekin—that's the girl . . . er . . . dog . . . um . . . thing . . . I saw eating lipstick at the mall."

"Don't worry," Freekin said, taking his beloved's hand for a moment to give it a gentle pat.

Pretty pushed up the sleeves of her jumper. And in that moment, she seemed to grow about ten feet tall and ten feet wide. Her eyes spun and smoke rose from the top of her head. Fire blasted out of her mouth as she threw back her head and yelled at the top of her lungs:

"GOOGALIBAZIKELZIKELBABALOOBABA-LOOBABALOO!"

"Cha-cha-cha," Scary added softly.

Sophie snickered even more loudly, if anything.

"Oh no," Freekin and Lilly said at the exact same time.

"GOOGALIBAZIKELZIKELBABALOOBABA-LOOBABALOO!"

"Cha-cha-cha."

Sophie's snickering slowed.

"It's working," Freekin said hopefully.

Then Pretty took a huge, deep breath, practically sucking all the oxygen out of the air. Her lungs filled. Her tentacles puffed up. Her eyes cartwheeled in her face.

"GOOGALIBAZIKELZIKELBABALOOBABA-LOOBABALOO!"

"Cha-cha-cha," Scary finished in a very soft whisper.

Sophie stopped snickering. She got to her feet, walked over to Freekin, and laid her head against his side.

"Sophie!" Freekin exclaimed as he got on his knees to

hug his dog. "Good girl, good girl, I knew you could do it." He patted her back and she got up on her feet and panted heavily. Her tail wagged back and forth as she furiously licked her master's cheek. "Aw, Sophie-girl," he said, wiping a tear from his eye.

Then he stood up and turned to Pretty. "I don't even know how to thank you, Pretty. What would I have done without you?"

Pretty twirled in a circle. "Tra la la!"

"Oh Freekin," Lilly whispered. "You're the sweetest guy I know." She gazed up at him. Her eyes were gleaming. Her shiny red lips parted.

And he knew, as surely as he knew that Lilly was the only girl he had ever crushed on, that she was just about to kiss him.

It was what he had come back from the grave for, wasn't it? To be Lilly's boyfriend? To kiss the beautiful, wonderful Lilly Weezbrock?

He dipped his head, his lips hovering just above hers. Then he realized what he was doing, and jerked backward.

"AIEEEE!" Pretty screamed. "No Lilly!" she cried. She narrowed her eyes and began to growl.

"Pretty's right. Lilly, I can't," he told her. "You'll get sick. You might die."

"I think not," Raven interjected. "You never kissed Shadesse. Or Brad. Or any of the other unfortunates who are sick."

"Maybe I never kissed them. Or even shared the same bottle, like I did with Brad. Or was licked by any of them the way I was licked by Sophie. But maybe they all had contact with someone I had contact with first. That still means they got it from me."

"Wait. You think you're making everyone sick," Steve said.

Freekin nodded.

Steve shook his head. "No way, man. My aunt called this morning. My cousin in Minnesota has this. And he's all the way in Minnesota. In fact, he's never been out of Minnesota."

Everyone took a moment to absorb the news. The wind whistled through the trees. Sophie started digging on top of another grave.

"It's not me?" Freekin asked.

"Oh, please stop asking questions," Lilly begged. "You can go to the principal and say you're sorry, Freekin. You can promise that you'll never ask another question as long as you live."

He stared at her. "Lilly, don't you see? We should have been asking questions all along. You . . . you would have

kissed me without even stopping to ask if it was safe. You just saw Sophie have a Chronic Snickering attack after she licked my face. Don't you think you should have questioned whether it could happen to you?"

"Stop asking questions!" Lilly cried. "You've caused enough trouble. If you're going to be like that, Freekin, some . . . evil questioning guy, I don't even want to kiss you! Ever! I'm sticking with Brad."

She burst into tears and ran out of the cemetery.

As he watched her go, the wind whipped at his cheeks as if it was slapping him across the face for being such a fool. He realized that his ears had fallen off. His left foot was loose again. He was a mess.

Everything was a mess. His great life was a joke. He had been kicked out of school, his father had no job, and he had lost Lilly. Again.

He thought about his chart. He was back to square one. Negative square one.

"Listen, man," Steve said, as if he could read Freekin's mind. "You probably saved my life last Friday. I'm—I'm sorry I acted the way I did."

"I can't blame you," Freekin said, watching Lilly get smaller and smaller as she stomped through the graveyard. "If you had come to me like that, I would have freaked out, too."

"And you have my undying friendship," Raven intoned.

"Of all us goths," Tuberculosis said for the group. They nodded.

"Whatever you face, you can face it with us," Steve added. "We've got your back."

"And us!" Pretty announced, grabbing his hand and kissing it. "Pretty eats you back!"

"Gazeeeee!" Scary agreed, fluttering against Freekin's cheek.

"Pretty Freekin Scary!" Pretty shouted.

Sophie trotted over and dropped a skull at his feet.

"Woof," she said.

Freekin shot his friends a quick smile to show them how grateful he was for their support. But deep down, even though he knew he was looking out for Lilly and the citizens of Snickering Willows, in the best and most important of all ways, he hated himself for doing it. Hated what it could end up costing him.

And then, for the final time that day, he asked himself a question. *If I'm doing the right thing, then why does it have to be so freakin' hard?*

Chapter 14

In Which We . . . Give Me a Second . . . OK, Got It . . . In Which We Say Good-Bye for Now

✳ ✳ ✳

Hello, Gentle Reader. I was just rereading this manuscript when I realized that I ended my story with the inauspicious and most unlucky thirteenth chapter. I couldn't do that to my dear Freekin and his friends, especially while they're in the midst of such a precarious predicament. If anything happened to them, I would surely think it my fault and I could never forgive myself. For as I have mentioned several times before, I have grown quite fond of them all.

You'll have to forgive me, though, for penciling in this last chapter. I don't have a printing press at home, obviously, so I'm writing this in by hand. Although to be quite honest, I don't know what to write, because I don't yet know where the story goes from here. So bear with me please, while I try my hand at improvisation.

What about . . . and they all lived happily ever after?

No, that's not quite right.

How about a poem?

Roses are red,

Violets are . . . No, that won't work either.

I suppose I could tell a joke. But then again, I'm really not a very humorous person.

I know just the thing! I could use this opportunity to remind you one last time that when you're done reading this book, it would be greatly appreciated if you could inform the International Order of Narrators of how much you enjoyed my work! I admit, this last option is a little self-serving, but I don't see as how I have much of a choice under the circumstances. So, yes, Dear Reader, please, please, remember to contact the Order

of Narrators at your earliest convenience. You won't be sorry.

Thank you for your consideration.